The fresh air beckoned him forward and he reached the window. The light was already brightening, more gold than pink, and he squinted against the sky.

Below him, in the field, a dozen or so people were gathered. They were stood in the wheat, and Mike could see the long stalks came up to their chests and shoulders. There were perhaps twelve of them; Mike did not count. Although the morning was warm for a September, he could see that all of them had pulled their hoods over their heads against the cold. Was this part of the harvest festival?

Suddenly there was movement below. The figures did not move from their spots, but there came an animation over them, as if they had been standing to attention and were now at ease. Mike saw with a surge of panic that the figure opposite him looked straight up, straight at him. He averted his eyes quickly and moved from the window, wincing as he stepped too quickly on his injured ankle.

The eyes that had spotted him had been blue; arctic blue. Mike was sure of it…

Also by Liam Smith:

THE WITCHING HOURS

THE PATCHWORK CARNIVAL

THE GREATEST SHOW
UNDER THE EARTH

THE TAXIDERMIST AND OTHER GIFTS

Harvest House

LIAM SMITH

This is a work of fiction. Names, characters, businesses, places, events and incidents are either the products of the author's imagination or used in a fictitious manner. Any resemblance to actual persons, living or dead, or actual events is purely coincidental.

First published 2017

This edition 2023

Copyright © 2017 Liam Smith

Cover art © 2023 Neil Elliott and Liam Smith

Illustrations © 2023 Neil Elliott

Liam Smith asserts the moral right to be identified as the author of this work.

All rights reserved.

First printed Anno Domini 2017

ISBN: 9781548131487

Harvest House

Thanks to...

My family and friends. I love writing, but turning writing into stories wouldn't be possible without the feedback and corrections of my nearest and dearest. Thank you for all your time and support.

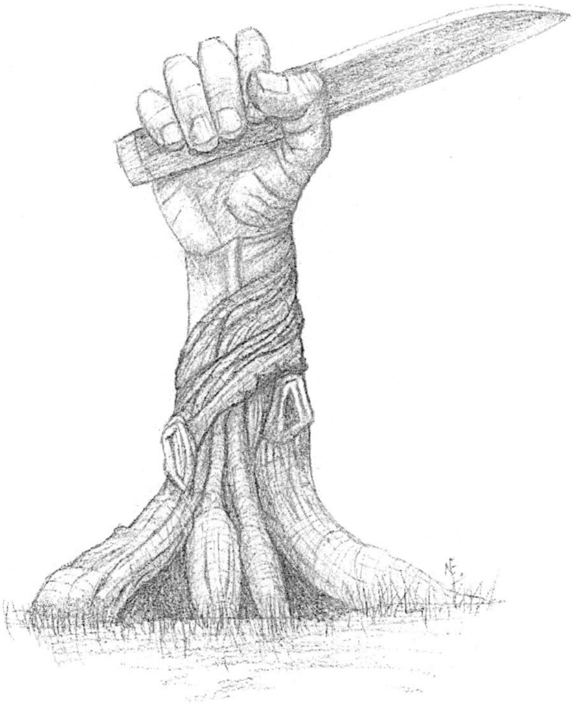

I

Green and gold spun past on either side of the road, whipped to a blur by the speed of the bike. Branches vaulted overhead, the afternoon sun flashing between fingery twigs. Birds wheeled beyond the hedges on both sides. The bike tyres hissed on the ground, the pedals clicking a steady cadence as they pumped up and down, up and down, up and –

WHUMP.

The trees overhead lurched and the hedges swung around. The road rose up and spun as the bike hit the ground and scraped along the tired tarmac. Then there was silence, save for the clicking of the back wheel as it spun against the gear like a clock in fast-motion.

Clickclickclickclickclickclick...

A gloved hand reached out and stopped the wheel. Then it rested, palm down on the ground, and tensed as its owner hauled himself up.

The cyclist looked behind him. Where was it? The animal he'd swerved to avoid? It had been a sheep or goat or something, stood on the left-hand side of the road. Right in his path.

He peered at the hedge and grunted as he put his weight on his left foot. Must be sprained. No, the creature was gone. It must have bolted; back through whichever chewed-through hole in the hedge had admitted it in the first place.

'Well, shit.'

The cyclist tried his luck on his left foot again, grunted, and hobbled to where his bike lay like a carcass on the ground. Not a sound rippled the air, but still – he pulled the bicycle to the grassy verge in case a car came zooming past. He propped it up on its handlebars and saddle. Spun the wheels.

Clickclickclick...

They weren't bent or broken. He tried the brakes, wincing as he knelt on his bad foot, and the wheels slid to a halt. Then it wasn't all bad.

The cap at the end of his left handlebar had come off and a spiral of foam had made a break from its home around the handle, crawling to freedom in a ribbon across the ground. There was some scratching there too, but nothing that wouldn't be covered up when the foam grip went back on. He'd need to hunt around for that cap –

His eyes caught sight of his pedals – well, pedal. The left one was just a steel rod, sticking out from the front cassette of gears.

'Shit.'

It must have sheared off as it scraped along the ground.

His eyes roved the road, locating the broken pedal over the other side. He checked both ways before crossing, though there were no cars to see. The pedal was cracked down its middle and he held it up, testing for any malleability in the plastic that might permit it to bend back into place.

A low rumbling came from behind him and a moment later a car zoomed past. Didn't offer any help. But then, would he? He supposed he wasn't really injured. And he wasn't expecting any sympathy. The Fiat disappeared around a bend a quarter-mile away.

Back to the bike. The pedal wouldn't snap back around the rod; God knew how it had come off in the first place. He checked his bag for anything useful, sifting through tyre levers, a pump, a small screwdriver and a Maglite. What he needed was some pliers; something to open up the pedal and then clamp it back onto the rod. But he hadn't packed for repairs; only maintenance. Only one thing for it: cycle on the steel rod. He couldn't be far from civilisation.

He flicked the bike over, back onto its tyres. It bounced a little with the suspension, and he leant on it, testing the sprain in his ankle. Somewhere overhead, a bird *cawwed*. The trees rustled.

He pulled himself onto the bicycle and set his right foot into the undamaged pedal. Without waiting, he pushed away, butting through the stab of pain that bit into his ankle. Gradually, the road began to roll beneath him.

The grimace on his face turned into a little smile. It felt like he was limping on the bike; he couldn't push down on the broken pedal-rod, only guide it round as he pumped with his right foot. He could already feel the strain in his right leg as it took on the share of the left. He hoped he didn't look as ridiculous as he felt.

Another car hummed in the distance behind him, the engine building to a roar as it swept past him. Golden-brown leaves twitched on the verges.

Towns in this part of the country were rarely more than a few miles apart. He could cover five miles in twenty-five minutes; he'd be able to find somewhere soon. Somewhere to collect himself, fix the bike as best he could until he could get hold of a new pedal. See, there – a turning. And beside it, a signpost.

He skimmed to a halt before the sign and put his right foot to the ground. Straight on would lead to a dual carriageway. The distance beside the little number read twenty-four miles. There were some larger towns on the sign too; they were even further away. Was there really nothing closer?

The turning led further into the southern countryside. There was only one name on the sign pointing down the tree tunnel there: Crookleton, two miles.

A car roved over the hill before him, ignoring the small turn-off and continuing down the main road.

That one had its sidelights on. The afternoon was drawing in.

The cyclist shrugged to himself and pushed away. He wobbled a little as his left foot scrabbled against the gripless rod, but found his balance and turned into the tree tunnel.

He hadn't noticed the sun was deepening in the sky till he'd seen those headlights, but under cover of trees the dimness was tangible. He leaned to click on his own lights; white at the front and flashing red at the back. His jacket was already a high-vis yellow, the better to reflect any light around. This was autumn – the most beautiful season, he reckoned, with its golden light, rusty trees and bonfire smells. It was worth the price of its shortening days.

Riding through the tunnel was like riding through a golden jewel box. The September sun glinted from falling leaves and mossy trunks, bright and earthy. The road was smooth, old but undamaged, and it whizzed beneath the bicycle tyres. It was just light enough that the bike's headlamp did not pool on the road before him, but melted into the autumnal glow. At this time in the afternoon, it would only help him to be seen – not to see the path ahead.

The wheat fields beyond the tree lines rolled like waves on the sea. The rush of a million stalks dancing in the evening breeze was shushed by his spinning wheels. As the sun slipped down another inch in the sky, the cyclist passed another sign. This one perched below a round, red-ringed speed limit.

Crookleton. Please drive carefully.

The road beyond seemed as empty as before, but now he could see the tree tunnel was reaching its end, opening onto the reddening sky. The dark masses of buildings were visible, clustered around the irregularly-shaped fields that canvassed this county.

The road began to move faster beneath the bike as a gradual downhill slope became apparent beyond the tree line. From up here, he could see the shape of the village below forming a wide letter V around a large wheat field, with the larger bulks of barns and sheds caught in the last rays of autumn sun. The fields continued, penned in by fences and hedges, down the slopes of the hill. The cyclist took his eyes from the vacant road and stood up on his remaining pedal to watch the fields fly past. At the base of the hill, the wavering carpet of wheat was broken by flattened areas, as if kids had been let loose in there and stomped their way around.

The road undulated and his stomach lurched as he zoomed up and down. He passed a few houses with big gardens, perched by the side of the road, and raised his arm to signal before turning down a street marked Crookleton Village.

It was a sweet place, in a rural English way. A few people were walking dogs along the high street and figures moved behind windows in the light of their homes. Many of the houses were one-storey cottages, ringed by low walls and flowerbeds. Longer driveways squeezed between the small houses, leading back to larger buildings behind. The cyclist passed a few junctions leading to cul-de-sacs and closes.

He'd passed no shops by the time he reached the end of the high street, though an MOT garage with some cars fanned across its forecourt lay opposite him now. Sighing, he turned left, following the other leg of the V-shaped village.

More houses. A community centre; an old stone building that looked more like a spireless church than a village hall. But there – a shop. And a pub fifty yards beyond it.

He pulled up outside the shop and hopped off the bike, wincing at the forgotten sprain in his ankle. He had a lock in a Velcro pouch beneath his saddle, but didn't bother to secure the bike. He would only be here a minute or two.

A small bell dinged as he opened the door, and he squeezed down a thin aisle of tins and magazines to reach the till. He nodded at the woman there, who returned the gesture with a thin smile.

'I wonder if you can help me,' he said. 'I'm cycling through – only it's getting a little dark and I wondered if there might be any accommodation around here. Or perhaps in a town nearby?' he added, observing the unchanging expression on the woman's face.

She remained silent for nearly half a minute, during which time her eyes strayed to the shop windows. The cyclist looked that way too, and saw himself reflected in the dark panes.

'There are no towns on the south road,' she said finally. 'Not for twenty miles or more. I don't know which road you bikled in on, but there's nothing on the south road.'

The cyclist quenched a smile – the woman had perhaps not intended her mispronunciation.

'I think I came that way. Down the hill, into the village.'

The woman looked at him over a bird-like nose. She was old, and the fluorescent lights of the shop planted cold half-moons in the spectacles perched on her beak. Behind them, the bell chimed as someone came in.

'If you follow the western road it'll take you to Dunkelton. It's a little larger than Crookleton. If it's a place to stay you're looking for, they have one of those –'

'Travelodges?' hazarded the cyclist.

'Homeless shelters.' The woman peered at him as if daring another interruption.

'Ah. I was thinking more something along the lines of a bed-and-breakfast.'

'Oh, but I can help you there.'

The cyclist turned. A chubby man with an armful of carrots plodded down the aisle.

'You can help?'

'Well, I run a bed-and-breakfast.'

'You're joking.'

Here, of all places.

'Absolutely. Beautiful village. Be a fool not to.'

The chubby man squinted at the till before plopping his carrots down. 'You staying a few nights?'

'I'm just passing through. Thought I might call it a night.'

'That yours out the front?' The chubby man nodded to the shopfront, where Mike's bike was propped.

The cyclist looked down at himself. His cycling jacket was bright under the lights.

'It is, yes.'

'It's missing a pedal.'

'I know. It happened earlier.'

The birdlike woman tapped the till.

'One pound and eight pence.'

'Thank you.' The chubby man picked up his carrots and turned to the cyclist. 'You want to come with me? House is just around the corner.'

The cyclist looked back at the old lady, and then back at the chubby man. He was already squeezing himself down the aisle towards the door. With a last nod to the woman, he followed his new friend and held the door for him.

'Thank you.'

The man began to plod away, leaving the cyclist to grab his bike and wheel it over.

'So what brings you to Crookleton?'

The man walked slowly but easily, carrots swinging by their stalks in one fist. He was leading them back to the high street. The odd streetlamp shone a glossy patch onto his balding head. His speech was monotone, flat whether he was asking a question or offering information, and slightly wheezing.

'I'm only passing through. I'm cycling somewhere.'

'Well you chose a good time. I had a cancellation I haven't been able to re-book. You can take that room.'

'You get many tourists here?' The cyclist was surprised. This was in the back-end of nowhere.

'Paragliders,' said the fat man. 'There's the centre up in Dunkelton. All the hills here; it's perfect for it. People like to make a weekend of it. We're in the middle of nowhere, you see.'

'I do.' Even without leaning on the bike, the cyclist's sprained ankle wouldn't have prevented him keeping pace with the chubby man. He was one of those slow-moving people town seemed to be full of on a Saturday afternoon.

'Then there are a few places to stay around here?' The cyclist didn't want to occupy the large man's puff with questions, but it helped him fight the urge to walk fast.

'Nope. I'm the only one outside of Dunkelton. I inherited the House many years ago; it's done me alright ever since.'

They passed the bend in the road opposite the MOT garage and set off down the high street.

'Lucky for me, then.' The cyclist flicked his lights off. No need for them now that he'd dismounted. 'To have bumped into you, that is.'

'Needed these for the pie.' The chubby man wiggled his fist of carrots. 'Here we are. Follow me.'

He pushed open a wooden gate and the cyclist followed him up onto one of the long driveways he'd seen from the road. They were approaching a large building; a cottagey-styled house. The walls were painted pale yellow, and the exterior was gridded with dark oak beams. A prism of thatch nested on the roof. A wooden sign, clearly homemade, was staked in the lawn.

Harvest House.

The chubby man led them to the front door, which sat in the middle of the house, between two windows. He knocked once on the door with an old iron ring before fiddling a key from his pocket and letting himself in anyway. The cyclist propped up his bike and followed him inside.

They passed through the thin entrance hall, straight into a room on the right. There was a desk there and the chubby man squished himself in behind it. The cyclist glanced around. This was a little sitting room – there were plump sofas, coffee tables and bookshelves straining with the weight of dozens of donated paperbacks.

'Just the one night, you say?'

'Yes please.'

'That's a shame. It's the start of the Festival tomorrow night. You'd be missing out.'

The cyclist smiled noncommittally.

'We'll see. Just the one for now.'

The chubby man jotted in a ledger.

'Payment is up front. If you want to stay another night, just let me know between now and then. Will you be paying by card or...'

The cyclist counted out notes from his wallet.

'Cash.'

The chubby man raised his eyebrows, but took the money.

'Right then. And your name?'

The cyclist tucked his wallet back into his rucksack.

'Michael Talbot. Mike.'

The chubby man wrote the name. Somewhere, a clock ticked.

'Good to meet you Mike. I'm Reece.'

'Pleasure.' Mike shook the proffered hand. It was like thrusting his fingers into a gammon.

'Here's your keys.' Reece held up a bunch of two, yoked to a carved wheatsheaf. 'That's your room key, and this big one is the front door key. Front door is locked after eight o'clock.'

'And where's my room?'

'Top of the stairs and left. Number five. If you can find your own way up, I'll wheel your bike into the hall.'

'That's very kind.'

Mike turned back into the hall and mounted the stairs. There was what appeared to be a breakfast parlour opposite the sitting room, but he climbed up past it, leaning on the banister to support his ankle. His legs burned from cycling, and he could almost feel the fibres in his muscles stretching and reknitting as he hit the landing.

A brass 5 was screwed to a door on his left. Opposite was a door with a 4. There were no other suites up here, only a few more unmarked doors that Mike took to be storage and boiler cupboards. He fed his key into the lock and unlocked the door to his room.

It looked comfortable; cosy even. Magnolia walls, soft brown bedcovers and curtains. Mike found the light switch to his left and a row of bulbs in a brass fitting sparked into life overhead. There was another door ajar to his right: that would be the en suite. Beside that door, a couple of wooden chairs nestled beneath a small coffee table, laden with a miniature kettle and a box of teas and coffees.

As Mike stepped inside, the door behind him shut with a clunk. He unclipped his rucksack and let it fall to the floor. He stretched, liberated of the weight, and crossed the room to the window. Though the light inside the room reduced the pane to an opaque glass panel, he cupped his hands around his eyes and stared out. He was at the side of the cottage – Harvest House – and he could see both the high street and the grey, rippling surface of the wheat field to the rear of the building. The room seemed very quiet –

There was a knock at the door.

Mike opened it a sliver, and Reece filled the tiny gap.

'I just wanted to let you know,' he said, 'I've brought your bike in. It's at the foot of the stairs. I imagine you usually lock it when it's outside, but it'll be safe enough in here.'

'Thanks very much.' Mike kept his fingers on the door handle.

'Then I'll leave you to it. Breakfast is between seven and nine. Come on down whenever you'd like.' Reece's eyes rolled up for a minute, as if trying to remember something else. 'Nope, that's it. I'll see you in the morning.'

'See you then.'

Mike shut the door and turned the little catch to lock it.

Here he was then: tonight's temporary residence.

He sat on the edge of the bed, then lay back. He felt the fatigue and the strain ebb from his body, pooling out and around him.

Another night. And then onward.

II

The shower was hot on his back, scalding his neck and shoulders. Steam rolled out from inside the curtained-off bath and made for the frosted-glass window, sticking to it in a thick veil of condensation.

Mike kept the heat up and ran his hands through his hair, working in the water and sluicing away the sweat from his cycling. He was a shower man. Could spend hours in there. But not in a bath: not soaking in his own filth. Showers were cleansing. Showers burned away the dirt and flushed it straight down the drain.

He worked his hands around his body, scrubbing hard as if stripping away the top veneer of skin. His flesh glowed lobster-red in the heat. When he was done, he turned off the taps and stood in the steam for a minute, letting the burn surrender to the colder air of his room. When he scrolled back the shower curtain and got out of the tub, he did not look at himself in the fogged-up mirror, only grabbed for a towel and dried himself, methodically, from his hair down to his feet.

In the bedroom, a mobile phone sat on the coffee table, its charging cable trailing down to a plug socket usurped from the kettle. The screen lit up as it charged, and notifications stacked up on the screen.

Mike wiped the mirror over the sink with his towel and ran hot water into the basin below. He unwrapped the complimentary soap and kneaded it to a lather, slathering the thin bubbles around his jaw. He pulled a razor from his small washbag and started to shave. When he was done, he splashed cold water over his face. He didn't have any aftershave.

Back in the bedroom, he pulled on fresh underwear and a pair of jeans. He limped his way over to the window and looked out again. The field was dark behind the house, but the high street glowed as streetlights and houses lit up for the evening. He sighed and lay back on the bed.

He'd run the bike up to the neighbouring village tomorrow. Dunkelton, was it? See if he could find a launderette and a bike shop. Hell, even a big supermarket might have pedals; they had everything these days. Clothes, TVs, toolkits... He'd be able to find something to get him moving again.

Moving onto...

Well. He'd soon find out, wouldn't he.

Something was ticking somewhere near his head. Mike looked over at a small travel clock on the bedside table. It was the kind that could fold up, clam-like, for transport, but for the present it was unfolded and propped up in his direction. The time read *7:31*. Nearly time for big Reece to lock up for the night.

Tick. Tick.

Mike leaned over, clamped the clock closed and stuck it in the drawer of the bedside table. Then he sat up and pulled a t-shirt on, pulling an open shirt on after it. He slipped his cycling trainers on and opened his door.

The landing was still. He hadn't heard any other guests around the house but there had to be a few – he was room number five, after all. Out of curiosity, he opened the unmarked doors. One was full of towels and linens. Another housed a large water cylinder. The last was locked.

He padded down the stairs, letting the banister take his weight when he stepped on his left foot. There was no one in the sitting room, and he passed straight out of the front door into the evening.

He could smell the country in the air; crops ripe and ready for harvest dancing on the breeze, fresh grassy air chasing away the greasy stink of exhausts and machines. The driveway was dark but he made for the gate at its end, spotting the Harvest House sign in a pool of second-hand light from a neighbouring cottage.

He limped on, pushing past the hot coals of pain that throbbed in his ankle. The injury wouldn't heal itself – the best thing to do was just to wear it back in.

He passed the garage and crossed the road to take a look at the forecourt. After all, he was in no rush, and his foot would appreciate a pause. The cars were all decent enough – clean, in good nick – but they were all fairly old. There were no registration plates from the last ten years here.

Mike shrugged and walked on. It felt good to get off the bicycle in the evenings; to go at a slower pace, to be a pedestrian, not traffic. He could feel that autumn breeze in his hair – hair usually long enough to slick with a little wax, and a little longer than that from lack of trimming. His shaved face felt raw.

He reached the village shop where he had met Reece and walked in. The same bird-like woman perched behind the counter. Mike delved further into the shop, following the lighthouse beacon of a pair of fridges that towered over the surrounding shelves. He picked himself out a couple of wrapped pasties and a Yorkie, adding an overpriced box of painkillers as he got to the till.

'Staying the night then.'

The woman scanned his items and placed them in a cheap plastic bag.

'Yes. Reece's B&B.'

The woman sniffed but did not speak again. Mike paid with a five-pound note and fed the few coins he received back into a charity pot by the till. The birdlike lady watched him to the door.

The pasties were alright; a bit lumpy. They

would have been better hot. Mike didn't have much of an appetite though, just ate to fuel himself until morning. He unwrapped the Yorkie last and munched it slowly, enjoying the solid ingots of chocolate. When he was done, he threw the wrappers in someone's wheelie bin.

The time was five to eight. Mike swiped away the notifications on his phone without looking at them and mooched onwards. He would go for a beer at the pub down the road and, around nine o'clock, head back to his room.

The pub was large: as big as Reece's cottage, only L-shaped. It had the same thatched roof and beamed facade, but a cluster of tables and parasols bustled outside, broadening its appearance. A couple of drinkers sat outside, and why not? It was a pleasant enough evening.

Mike walked in, letting the thick door with its iron knocker swing shut behind him. It was low-ceilinged in the pub with a flagstone floor, and tables at low and chest level were dotted around between the columns and buttresses in the walls. It smelled rich and hoppy, like sweet old beer and fermenting straw, and a decade of smoking ban hadn't been long enough to roust the last of a tobacco-y, leafy smell from the walls.

The bar sat at the hinge of the L-shaped space, looking out into both sections of the pub, and Mike made for it. There were a few drinkers around the pub, and bubbles of conversation burst sporadically against the low-level sound of a stereo playing old pop.

'What'll it be?'

'I...' Mike stared at the woman behind the bar. Save for the lack of half-moon spectacles, she could have been the shopkeeper's twin. 'A pint of bitter, please.'

'Of course.' The old lady blinked at him down the barrel of her beaky nose. 'You'll be here for the Festival, I take it.'

'Ah... no.' Mike watched the pump as the old woman heaved at it, jetting dark ale into a glass.

'A glider, then.' The old woman sniffed. 'Though I don't know why anyone would choose to do such a thing. These modern machines. Just because they've been invented, it doesn't mean there's a use for them. I suppose you've done it before.' She set the glass before him.

'Ah... no,' said Mike again.

'They come from all over the country, they do, to fly about here.' The woman rang the beer into the till but didn't ask for payment. Mike slipped a note from his wallet by the price on the till's display. 'Good hills for it, so I hear, but they watch the circles too, I know. I don't hold with it, it's not for human eyes, the goings-on down on the ground, not from up there at any rate. Still, the weather's holding out, so they won't be put off. Thank you.'

Mike grabbed his pint before the woman could resume her chatter, and walked it around the bar. He could see a pair of patio doors and the vague shape of outdoor furniture beyond. He looked back at the bar, where the birdlike woman watched him whilst dragging a rag across the wooden bar, shaking her head ever so slightly.

He picked his way out into the balmy evening and set himself down at a table. He was the only one out here. His pint simmered by his hand and he took a gulp, drinking past the thin head of foam and into the body of the beer. It had a stewed flavour, but it wasn't unpleasant. It was full and dark, and tasted as if there was some fruit hidden in its depths somewhere.

Mike wasn't a cider drinker and he didn't enjoy summery, citrusy beers. But this was fine. This would do him for now. He popped a couple of painkillers from their packet and washed them down with the beer.

The pub's garden backed onto the same wheat field as Reece's B&B. Mike couldn't see through the evening gloom, but he could guess where Harvest House was situated, between the middle of the high street and the garage on the junction. Overhead, a parchment-white moon was rising into a star-scattered sky. It was brighter out here than near the city; it lit up the hedges and rooftops and trees with a pale light instead of just hanging in the sky like a spent coin.

Mike took another drink. The field rustled, the ears of wheat quivering in a low breeze, illuminated by the moon. There were no streetlights to the rear of the pub and houses. It was refreshing, tranquil and natural. He could see the couple of patches in the field where the crops had been flattened nearby. Maybe the kids were playing at flying saucers. He'd done that kind of thing as a kid; been chased from fields by farmhands after cutting the ties on hay-bales. He wondered if the kids had gotten away with it or if they'd been caught and threatened with a beating or – worse – a word with their parents. A thin smile twitched his lips. He took another swig of beer.

Crookleton didn't look big enough to have its own festival. Perhaps it was an ale festival – perhaps there were suppliers over in that town, Dunkelton, who flogged their wares over here. Maybe it was just a car boot sale, held in some unseen car park or field. It didn't matter. He wouldn't be around to see it.

Bzzz.

His phone vibrated in his pocket. Mike took another swig of beer and ignored it. Now that he was halfway through the pint he wasn't sure if he did like it. It sat in his belly like tar and dried his mouth out like a sponge. All the more reason to leave in the morning. Couldn't trust a place with bad beer.

He drained the last of it, scrunching his face as the dregs went down. He stood up, a little light-headed from the drink, and returned to the pub. The sprain in his ankle niggled at him, but he kept his steps firm and purposeful. He plonked the glass down on the bar.

'Same again?'

The old woman peered at him. She had to be the other woman's twin. She was identical in appearance, but she had clearly inherited the lion's share of talking genes.

'No. Thank you.' Mike headed for the door.

'See you again,' called the woman. The few other drinkers watched as Mike left the place.

He kept his gait steady till he'd passed the shop, then began to limp shamelessly as the pain flared up, undiminished by the tablets he'd taken. There was no point pushing it too far – he had to cycle on it tomorrow. A couple passed him on the other side of the street and he could see someone on a nocturnal stroll ahead of him, but there weren't many people about. He made it back to Harvest House, letting himself in the front door and nearly tripping over his bike. No one was around to see him.

Back in his room, he stripped off to his boxers and lay back on the bed. He skimmed a finger across his phone screen, wiping away the notifications. Then he lay back into the pillows, with the pain of his ankle throbbing hot and soft, and let the darkness take him.

III

'Mmmmmph.'

Mike rolled over then lay still. His head hurt.

What? That wasn't fair. He couldn't be hungover from one pint. It had been a dodgy pint though, hadn't it? It mustn't have agreed with him.

Light squirreled its way around the edges of the curtains, golden and bright. A sunny morning; more like summer than autumn. Mike didn't get photosensitive when he was hanging; good job too.

What was...

A shred of sleep-memory fluttered by like a leaf caught in a breeze. He'd dreamed something; second-hand images came to him of running, running on his sprained foot through – what? – alleyways? Tunnels? He couldn't remember. Had there been fire in the dream?

But it was slipping away. Gone. No matter. Mike liked to remember what he could in dreams – try to pin parts of them to what must have inspired them the previous day. Clearly, his foot must have been distracting his mind in the night. He looked down at the foot, pulling the covers away. It looked a little swollen, but not too bad.

He got out of bed, limped a little, and made it to the bathroom. He pissed out a dark stream while kneading his temples between his thumb and middle finger. The light filtering through the frosted glass of the wide bathroom window was strong and yellow – just what time was it? He washed his hands as the toilet flushed, rinsing the sleep from his eyes, and returned to the bedroom without drying his face. He looked at his phone.

11:58.

No. It couldn't be.

As he watched, the phone's display ticked on another minute.

Shit. He was an early riser by nature – he'd never slept this long before, not unless he'd come home at five in the morning from a night out. He must have been out of it for ten hours or more!

'Shit...'

He'd had plans for the morning. He'd intended to make it to the neighbouring town, fix his bike up then be on his way, cycling on. Now that plan was scuppered. What day was it? Friday. He could still get the bike fixed. The shops would be open.

He hauled his clothes on and his stomach grunted. He'd have missed Reece's breakfast. Have to get himself something in town. What an idiot.

He packed his clothes and his few accessories into his rucksack and located the room key on its wheatsheaf ring. He padded down the stairs, past where his bike sat in the hallway. He got to the front parlour and approached the little desk. There was a brass bell there, and he tapped it hesitantly. It *dinged* loudly in the quiet house.

There came a creaking from somewhere up above, and Mike followed its trail as it turned to heavy footsteps on the staircase. A moment later Reece appeared in the doorway.

'Mr Talbot. Good afternoon.'

Mike groaned inside at that word.

'Afternoon Reece. Just wanted to say thanks for the room.' He held out the keys.

'You missed breakfast, you know.' Reece didn't move from the doorway. 'Heavy night, was it?'

'Think the cycling caught up with me. There's been a couple of weeks of it.'

'Well, that's understandable.' The chubby man's tone wasn't hostile. 'Will you be moving on then?'

'After I get my bike fixed.'

'Where are you cycling to?'

'Just... onwards.' Mike proffered the keys again. 'Thanks very much.'

This time Reece took the keys.

'You'll be cycling to Dunkelton for the bike, I presume.'

'So it would seem.'

'Well,' Reece puffed his chest out. 'If you're late back, the room will probably still be available. It's the start of the Festival tonight as well. Could be worth your time to stop around.'

'Thanks very much.' Mike made a non-committal nudge of his head, halfway between a nod and shake. 'I'll see what time I'm up and running.'

'Good man.' Reece moved out of the doorway. 'Then I'll let you get away.'

Mike edged past him, got to his bike and wheeled it out onto the driveway. He looked back, and Reece raised a hand in farewell before closing the door.

At the high street he mounted the bike and pushed away to the right. The broken pedal and his painful foot made for a poor combination, and when he reached the main road his right leg was already aching from the extra strain. He pulled out nonetheless, forgetting the discomfort as he fell into the task of moving himself forward. He passed a sign for Dunkelton – five miles – and took heart. He'd be there in half an hour.

It was a pleasant enough ride, if marred by his limping attempts at cycling. The air was a little breezy, but not enough to push him around, and the skies were clear. Hedges at the roadside corralled fields of crops; most of them stubbly after the harvest. Hills rolled around him, though the slope of the road never ramped beyond a gentle rise.

To his amusement he spotted a few gliders in

the sky – perhaps they were staying with Reece at Harvest House. It was a stunning day for it. What had the barmaid said last night? The hills were good for it. Well, he could see why. He imagined launching himself from one of those peaks, riding the wind with a patchwork of fields and model railway-sized villages below. Would he have the balls to do it? He wasn't afraid of heights. Sure; he could give it a go one day.

What else had the woman in the pub said? *They watch the circles.* He hadn't known what she'd meant last night, and he was none the wiser now. But the phrase, dredged from his memories, seemed to resonate with him.

They watch the circles.

What circles? He looked to the sky at the pair of gliders, swooping like birds against white flecks of cloud. A flash of sensation came to him; of running, running on his throbbing foot, running through –

A car passed on the other side of the road.

It was gone.

*   *   *

He reached Dunkelton around one o'clock. He passed through a border of trees and followed the road as it led past a few converted farm buildings and smaller houses. As he went on, wheels skimming, freewheeling on a downhill stretch, smaller roads started peeling from the main. There were houses, a village green with a playpark and a pair of goalposts, a cricket pavilion. He reached the main street of shops and swung himself from the bike, pushing it as he joined the pedestrians on the pavement.

Dunkelton was small but had decent enough facilities. There were a couple of restaurants up here, a couple of takeaways. A miniature incarnation of a chain supermarket lurked on the other side of the road but the other small businesses seemed to be independent: a barber, a stationer, a doors and windows store, a running and cycling shop. Mike made for the latter and locked his bike around a lamppost outside.

He picked out a fresh set of pedals, cheap enough but not too cheap, and took them to the counter.

'Is that yours?' The shopkeeper nodded at his bike outside.

'Yep.'

'Would you like me to fit the pedals?' The shopkeeper was over the hump of middle age, but looked fit enough. He moved quickly and purposefully, and Mike imagined him cycling everywhere every day.

'I should be alright. Thank you though.'

'You know, if you've far to go...' The shopkeeper glanced at the bike outside. 'It could be worth a service.'

'A service?'

'Lubricating your gears, checking tyre pressure, aligning your gears and brakes...' he paused. 'Washing the bicycle.'

They looked together at the bike. A pebbledashing of brown splattered the blue aluminium.

'How long will it take? Only I've got somewhere to be.'

'Two hours or so.' The shopkeeper raised a pair of thick, iron-grey eyebrows. 'I think it could be worthwhile.'

Mike checked the time on his phone.

'Okay,' he said. 'I think I can squeeze it in.'

He unlocked the bike and wheeled it into the shop, trading it for a business card with a time biroed on its reverse.

He found a launderette beside the barber's salon and dumped his change of clothes in a washing machine. A wash and dry would fill most of the time his bike needed. He left his laundry and headed back out, wandering up the slope of the high street, trying to acclimatise to his sprain. It was best to get the bike fixed. He'd ridden it a lot and planned to do so for many more miles; it would pay itself back. In the meantime, he'd take a stroll uphill and see if he couldn't take in the view.

The street led to a small housing estate, but opposite the ranks of seventies-looking semi-detached houses was a clump of woodland with a carpark and footpath signs. He made his way through the carpark and along a bridleway, feeling for the gradient of the hill as he aimed for the top. The forest was fresh and woody-smelling; pinecones crunched under his feet and leaves flitted down from the trees. The uneven ground was uncomfortable but he stuck with it. It would be worth it for that view.

When he did emerge from the trees ten minutes later, it was everything he'd hoped for. He put his hands on his thighs as he breathed in the air – the last push uphill had taken his wind – and gazed around.

The hill sloped down at a steep gradient from where he was now. He could imagine barrel-rolling down; it would take minutes to reach the bottom and would be enough to make any man sick. The slope rose into further hills, ebbing and flowing like a storm on a green, frozen ocean.

Further around the crest of his hill he saw a low, modern looking building. As he watched, a couple of figures rounded it with gliding equipment. They got to the edge of the hill and, after a few minutes, dove from the top. Mike watched them zoom away, instructor and passenger hanging from the fragile set of wings.

He could see Crookleton from here. The strangely shaped village bent around on a flatter plain in the hills. He could follow the grey snaking road that he had ridden in on through the village, up to the tree tunnel he had first navigated the previous day. The fields were spread out in the flat basin, taking advantage of the level ground. He could see the wheat field that nestled in the angle of the V-shaped streets of Crookleton. It was strange that the field had not been harvested yet; he could see many of the fields around had been cut for their produce, reduced to bristles and mud.

He could just about pinpoint where the village pub was, and he scanned for Reece's Harvest House. But he was too far away, and the house blended into the streets despite its size. Then he noticed the circles.

They watch the circles.

Is this what the bar lady meant? The two stamped-down patches in the field? Looking now, he could see the dark sections of field might well be circles; not arbitrarily flattened patches as he had first thought. Was there something wrong with the earth that meant the wheat couldn't grow there? Or had they been levelled on purpose?

Perhaps it was some local nut, he mused, making his own crop circles. Maybe he'd been in the local rag, famous for it. That was the kind of thing that happened in these places, wasn't it? A little oddity; a quirky attraction in the county.

The paragliders were smaller in the sky now, shrunk by distance. They would have had a good view of the circles. He supposed he might later; it would be mid-afternoon by the time he was done in town, and the road signs for Dunkelton hadn't promised any likely stops within an hour's ride or so. Maybe he should cut his losses – stay another night in Harvest House and ride out early in the morning. He couldn't imagine setting out now. He'd lost the immediacy that came with setting out at first light, and the autumn sun would quickly reduce him to cycling by night. Not ideal on these country roads.

He sighed. His laundry would be nearly done.

Time to head back to civilisation.

He picked his way back through the woodland. His ankle was feeling better; sore but without the pulsing heat that had plagued him earlier. When he returned to the launderette he found there were ten minutes left on the dryer's clock. He waited on an uncomfortable plastic seat, swaddled in the smell of hot washing powder, before throwing his change of clothes into a plastic bag and stuffing that into his rucksack.

At the bike shop he traded sixty pounds for a clean, shining blue bicycle.

'Tyres pumped, pedal fixed, brakes adjusted, batteries in your lights changed.' The bike seller wheeled Mike's bike to the front of the shop. 'Far to go this afternoon?'

'Back to, ah, Crookleton.' Mike gesticulated in the village's direction as he tucked his wallet back into his bag. 'Just down the hill.'

'Oh, I know Crookleton.' The man's eyes were very dark, Mike noticed now. Shiny, like spots of oil. 'You're visiting for the Festival.'

'Just passing through.' Mike turned to go, then turned back, rolling his eyes at himself for surrendering. 'What is this festival?'

The man smiled. There was salt-and-pepper stubble on his jaw, and it tweaked as his mouth did.

'We hold a yearly celebration,' he said. 'At the Scythe and Stack. Food, drink, music. Every autumn.'

'The Scythe and Stack?'

'The public house.'

'Ah.' Mike contained a grimace as he thought of his head that morning. 'It attracts many tourists, then? The festival?'

'Not usually. No, it's more of a local activity.'

'Okay.' Mike nodded. 'And you'll be there?'

'Absolutely. I live in Crookleton.' The man smiled again. 'If you're staying the night, you should join us.'

'I'll see what I'm doing.' Mike nodded. 'Thank you.'

'Enjoy the ride back,' said the man. 'Downhill all the way.'

Mike nodded again and left the shop.

IV

Mike enjoyed the ride back to Crookleton. With his pedal fixed, the ground had fairly flown past, and he'd shot into the high street without a thought of his uncomfortable ankle. He'd grabbed a late lunch in Dunkelton too; a sandwich and a coffee. He hadn't eaten all day, despite missing breakfast, and it was restorative to feel something in his belly.

It was still light when got back to Harvest House, and on impulse he left his bike and rucksack in the hallway. There was nobody in either front room, though he heard some movement from upstairs, and he strolled back outside with just his keys in the pocket of his cycling shorts.

He would take a look at the wheat field.

He rounded the side of the house – opposite to the side his room was on. He wondered if Reece had stripped and cleaned the room yet; for that matter, if he'd had a last-minute booking. Well, he'd find out soon enough.

There was a car parked round the side of the house: a five-door saloon. Behind that was a tall fence and gate. Mike unlatched the gate and it creaked open onto a small but well-tended garden. There was a paved area with some cast iron furniture and a vibrant green lawn. A few slim trees at either side helped enclose the garden from its neighbours, but a low fence at the back allowed an uninterrupted view of the field.

Mike stepped across the patio and onto the grass.

The sea of wheat shimmered before him, all soft and golden. He could smell it too; an earthy, natural smell that reminded him of running down country lanes as a kid. Running...

Again, that sensation, that dream-memory of running on his stabbing ankle through...

And it was gone again.

Mike was no stranger to nightmares – not after the last few weeks. But this one had sunk its barbs in deep. He shook his head.

He could see a round patch in the field; a circle, if that's what it was. It was perhaps twenty feet from the perimeter and another thirty from one side to the other. It looked round from where he was standing, but he couldn't see if it had been flattened or mown or if there had never been any growth there at all. There were channels in the field too – tracks crushed in by the heavy wheels of a tractor as it had rumbled around, sowing or spraying or whatever it was that tractors did.

He was curious. What was so special about this place? Why the circles?

'Afternoon Mike.'

Mike turned. Reece was lumbering across the lawn. He wore an apron – it hugged his body to his belly, then dropped straight down the overhang like a waterfall.

'Afternoon Reece.' Mike looked around at the garden. 'Sorry. Didn't mean to trespass.'

'I spotted your bike in the hallway.' Reece's hands were in his pockets. He gazed out across the field. Mike could hear his breathing; steady but deep. Overweight breaths. 'Figured you must have come back for the room.'

'Would that be alright?' Mike sought to catch his eye, but Reece was staring out beyond the fence. Neither man spoke for nearly half a minute.

'Sorry.' Reece blinked and looked around. 'Away with my thoughts. Yes, the room's free. It'll be a pleasure to have you.'

'I appreciate it. It's short notice.'

'Not a problem. Payment upfront. Breakfast till nine, if that's not too early.'

'I'm usually an early riser –' Mike stopped himself. The chubby man was only making a joke. 'I'm sure I'll make it tomorrow. Thank you.'

'Then this is for you.' Reece picked the wheatsheaf and its pair of hanging keys out of his apron pocket. 'I put your rucksack behind the desk in the parlour. In case anyone just walked in.'

'That's very kind.' Mike stepped back towards the house. Then he turned. 'Reece. What are the circles in the field?'

For a minute, Reece didn't reply – only looked out to the field again.

'They're for the Festival,' he said, finally. Mike waited, but Reece did not speak again. So he shrugged, and retreated to the house.

He showered again, scrubbing his skin red raw. Steam billowed out of the open bathroom door. When he was done, he wiped a clean patch in the mirror, and shaved away the thin grit of stubble that had fought its way onto his skin.

Reece hadn't deep-cleaned the room. True enough; the bed was made and the towels changed, but Mike found the travel clock still folded in the drawer, and a few coins on the small coffee table that he'd forgotten about had not been touched. It was as if he had never checked out.

It was only five o'clock. The sun was setting, bathing the field in an amber glow, and a cool draught sneaked in through the open window. Mike didn't mind. He preferred the fresh air. Too often he woke in the night, sweaty and with the duvet tangled around him. Better to have the air: he could always wrap himself tighter in the covers.

It was too early to go to bed – too early by far. He'd planned to cut his losses and replenish his energies tonight, ready for a long cycle in the morning, but for now he was left with nothing to do. He checked his phone, swiped away some waiting text messages, and grunted.

He had hours to kill.

A walk? No, not in the dark, not when the only place to walk was the unlit countryside.

The bus? He could take a ride to Dunkelton, see what it had to offer on an evening. But had Crookleton even got a bus-stop?

The pub?

Mike huffed to himself.

The festival at the pub tonight – that's what all the locals seemed so excited about. What had the bloke at the bike shop said? Food, drink and music? And Reece – he'd said the circles were for the festival.

Mike went to the window and looked out across the field. He couldn't see any activity, but then he was facing in the wrong direction. He was torn – the beer last night had soured his impression of the pub, but all the mention of tonight had ingrained in his consciousness as effectively as repeated adverts on the telly.

He looked at the little table with its miniature kettle. His rucksack was open on the floor beside it. A change of clothes spilled out. He had nothing else to do.

With another grunt, he turned from the window, collected his wallet and keys from the table, and left his room. Behind him, the open curtains twitched as the autumn breeze crept in at his window.

*   *   *

He enjoyed the walk to the pub. He had not stayed an extra night at any town yet and the familiarity after so many weeks was pleasing to him. He passed the garage and the village shop before getting to the pub.

Now that he paid attention, he noticed the pub sign that hung from its own post in front of the building. The Scythe and Stack, the man in the bike shop had called it. The gently swinging sign showed a big yellow pile of hay with a scythe propped against it, its blade to the ground. It was one of those curved implements Mike had seen more often at Halloween, in the hands of costumed grim reapers. He shivered involuntarily and headed for the front door.

Sounds of merriment and chatter bubbled around him as soon as he stepped inside. The bar was well lit and the fullness of the place made it seem brighter and more colourful than it had last night. No one took notice of Mike as he edged through the crowds milling around, though everyone seemed in high and happy spirits. Men in chequered shirts drank beer and cider from tankards, and women laughed and chattered. Mike couldn't be sure if there was even any music on in the background; the volume of noise from the congregation was too high.

He made it to the bar, waiting for a train of middle-aged couples to wind past him towards the garden.

'Back again?' The bar lady peered at him. 'Enjoyed your stay at Reece's, did you?'

'Apparently so.' Mike held up a hand as she made for a familiar ale pump. 'What else do you have?'

'Didn't you like the bitter?' She didn't wait for a reply. 'A local one that — well, of course they're all local, something of an acquired taste. Others — visitors — don't seem to take to some of them. Well, it's their loss, and they rarely stay for long anyway, only long enough to —'

'What else do you have on?' Mike made room for someone else at the bar.

'I'll pull you a Strange.'

The bar lady swapped the glass for a handled pint tankard and turned to a keg behind her, lying on its side. She twisted the spigot and a slightly fizzy, dark amber concoction poured out.

'What is it?' Mike looked at the tankard as it was placed in front of him.

'Strange,' she said. Then she was taking another order, chattering away to a man next to him. He shrugged and tried the pint. It was decent; easier to drink than the bitter had been. It tasted a bit more citric, a little fruity, but not appley enough to be cider. It was almost certainly the output of some nearby bumpkin brewery. Not usually his thing, but good enough.

He left the bar. It was noisy in the pub and not unpleasantly so, but tonight he was a solo drinker.

Having so much cacophony didn't suit his mood. Instead, he made for the garden. On his way he passed a nook that had remained empty. A few stools were set up there and a few cases were propped against the wall. *Food, drink and music.* Here was the music. Not a soft rock tribute band then. Probably some folksy flower group.

He got outside. It was busy out here too; chatting groups of men and women clustered about, and a few younger men lurked at the bottom of the garden, looking out over the field. Even in the failing light, Mike could see a shadowy patch where the field's second circle must lie. There weren't many people smoking, but Mike stifled a smile at the sight of an elderly man in a flat cap puffing away at a large pipe.

He wandered towards the younger men, more to find a spot away from familial groups then to eavesdrop, and settled his tankard on a fence post.

'There it is,' one man was saying. He was smoking: Mike could smell the tobacco. 'Just coming up now.'

Mike turned to see what they were looking at. The moon was rising as the sun went down, plump and ivory-yellow.

'Lovely clear night,' another man replied. 'It'll be a bright one.'

Mike smiled to himself again. No one would be found discussing the moon back where he lived. He barely noticed it himself; the stars were fairly obliterated by light pollution, and he'd never thought about moonlight as real illumination when there were streetlights down every road.

Not that moonlight is light from the moon, he thought to himself, dredging the fact out from several years of hibernation. *It's light from the sun, reflected by the moon.* He smiled again, more broadly this time, and took another swig of the Strange brew.

The night edged on. When Mike finished his pint he returned to the bar and ordered another.

'There's food too,' the bar lady said, nodding over to the right of the pub. Mike peered but couldn't see anything. When he received his pint he squeezed over to see what she had meant.

A few tables had been shoved together against one wall, and they were laden with plates and platters. Loaves of bread were cut into thick slices, and wheels of cheese, stacks of cured hams and joints were piled on dishes. Bowls of fruit polkadotted the spread and, as he watched, Mike saw two women pile some plates with bread, cheese and apples, and take them back through the crowd.

A free buffet?

Mike clicked – the festival. A harvest festival. That's what this was all about.

Harvest festivals didn't really exist back in town. Mike remembered signs outside churches advertising events around the autumn; usually charity affairs, collecting food for the homeless. He supposed these things were celebrated differently around the country – the people here probably relied on the local produce a lot more than city-slickers like him.

He left the food table and propped himself up at the bar, turning away from the loquacious bartender to avoid the torrent of chatter that engulfed any customers that approached the counter. He wasn't much of a people watcher though, and was relieved to see some activity over in the previously-empty nook. A couple of men and a woman were unpacking the cases that lay there, and setting up stools and equipment. This must be the band.

Mike had played guitar himself years back. He'd been alright. It had fallen by the wayside in recent years though, and other things had taken over. He'd lost the time and then the inclination to keep it up.

There were no guitars in the band corner though; Mike saw with a mixture of horror and amusement that what he had taken for a guitar case actually housed a lute. Its player was tuning it, turned away from the crowd to concentrate better. Beside him, his bandmate had unpacked a fat drum, the kind with strings criss-crossing it around the side. Both men were getting on a bit, judging by their matching iron-grey hair. Just what he needed – a geriatric folk trio. Well, it was something to do on a Friday night. He'd watch them for a set then head back to his room.

The woman with the two old boys had been bent down over a case on the floor, but now she stood up. Mike felt a small frisson of surprise pull at his chest.

She wasn't old at all; she was young. Younger than him; late twenties perhaps, or early thirties. She had long, white blonde hair that fell straight down to the small of her back, and her face was pale, made paler by the reds and oranges of the dress she wore. She had high cheekbones and blue eyes, and Mike saw her fingers were long, punctuated with red-painted nails as they danced across the shaft of a wooden flute she was holding to her lips.

Her eyes met his and he looked away, taking a sip of his pint.

The drummer patted his instrument a few times with his hand, testing the sound. The lutist turned around, his strings tuned, and Mike saw it was none other than the man from the bike shop. He watched as he played a few chords on the bulbous instrument, the sound glimmering through the buzz of chatter in the pub. It sounded a little like a twelve-string guitar and a little like a harp. Mike was intrigued despite himself.

Their checks done, the band placed their instruments on the tables around them and edged their way towards the bar. Mike turned from them, back towards the front of the pub, and found himself face to face with Reece.

'Evening Mike,' rumbled the fat man. 'You made it.'

'So it would seem.' Mike held up his glass. 'Can I, ah, buy you a drink?'

'No need.' Reece caught the attention of the bar lady and was handed a tankard a moment later, without any payment. 'They know me. Us small businesses stick together.'

Mike found himself torn. He had not come here for conversation; had not started riding his bike again to talk to people along the way. But part of him did long for a sense of companionship. It had been weeks since he'd left town; weeks on his own. Now, he didn't know whether he wanted to break that solitude or maintain it.

'Looks like I got here just in time.' Reece nodded over to where the band were returning to their nook, drinks in hands. Both the bike-man and the drummer had pints of Strange clutched in their hands, but the woman had a healthy measure of some amber spirit in a smaller glass. They reached their corner and the drummer and lutist settled themselves on high bar stools. The woman stood before them both and, after a sip of her drink, put the flute to her lips.

It began with a slow, rolling beat. The drummer used both his hands on the tight drum, beating out a wave of notes that merged with the noise of the pub before rising above it, till its presence was noticed by everyone in the place. The lutist joined in as the chatter of conversation fell to a lower whisper, plucking and picking at the strings and weaving a folksy, shimmery web of notes around the drum. The young woman began to play her flute, her painted nails creeping up and down the pipe as the high, mellow sound cut above the other instruments.

Mike found himself examining the woman's face again. Her features were Germanic, he thought:

light and fair. There was a flower in her hair, pinning it back on one side behind the shell of her ear. As she played her flute she swayed, and the dress she wore swayed with her, floating around her, enveloping her. Her eyes found his again and again he looked away, watching the lute-player's fingers spider across the strings.

The sounds of clinking glasses and plates, murmured conversation and laughter from outside still permeated the pub, but the trio of players had the attention of the majority. Then the flute held one long note and the lute's last chord faded as the drums rolled to a halt. There was quiet for a moment, the audience began to clap. Mike placed his tankard on the bar to join in and made to catch Reece's attention, but his landlord was still staring at the band, podgy hands thumping together. The woman took a bow as the men behind her nodded in thanks. Then she placed the flute to her lips again.

'They're not bad,' said Mike to Reece, but the chubby man wasn't listening.

The flute began to sing, but instead of the long and languid notes of the last piece, the woman began to play a staccato rhythm; short blasts with only the occasional held notes. Such a different style of playing changed the timbre of the instrument; it sounded dry and woody, like the wind howling through leafless trees. Mike took a gulp from his tankard.

The flute-player held a note, and the drums and lute joined in with a crash. The drummer held a quick, thudding beat and the lutist played his instrument like a guitar, strumming out a rhythm to match the percussion. The flute wheeled above them both, jabbing and dancing. It was raucous and fiery, the players nodding and stomping along to the music, the blonde-haired woman dancing fast.

Mike found his own foot tapping up and down in time. He would never have chosen a folk band to watch, but after two pints of strange brew and two weeks of non-stop cycling, he was starting to enjoy it. He drained his tankard and twisted around to order another. For once, the bar lady was quiet, and poured his drink from the cask without a salvo of chit-chat.

The people standing around the pub were already beginning to move to the beat of the music. Mike was surprised; live music in the pubs back at home rarely got people dancing before ten o'clock, and now it was just gone seven. He supposed it was their special, local festival – who knew how early the townsfolk had started? They were probably all well away.

He returned his gaze to the flute player. He couldn't help but stare at her; her dancing and playing was otherworldly, and her white face, flushed now from the heat and her movement, was beautiful. Mike felt that pull in his chest again, a pull of attraction. He let it swell for a moment, imagined in a second the rush of kissing her red lips, of feeling her pale body hot against his...

No. He gulped at his pint and averted his eyes.

He watched the lutist play; trying to spot familiar shapes as the man's fingers scurried about the strings. It was times like this that he missed playing his guitar. It was still around at home, stood in a corner of the spare bedroom, all unused and dusty. More a decoration now than an instrument. He hadn't touched it in years.

Drums – he'd never understood them. He watched the drummer now, hands slapping away at the thick skins, feet pumping up and down. One leg had a tambourine lashed around it; he could hear it steady in the music. How? How could anyone hold down two or three different rhythms at once like that? He could barely tap a foot in time with his own playing.

When – whenever – he returned to his house, he'd try and pick up the old six-string again.

The band played for another half hour or so. By the time they had finished, the air was thick and hot with movement. People had danced, young and old, holding hands and spinning with each other. Slops of beer spattered the floor.

There was a rush at the bar and Mike felt himself pinned to his spot by the weight of the crowd. He'd never experienced so excitable a group – not one so early, and so full of older people. What were they putting in the Strange?

'Good to see you Michael.'

Mike turned. It was the man from the bike shop; the lutist. His bandmates were behind him, ordering at the bar. Mike switched his eyes from them

– her – and nodded in greeting.

'Yes. And you.' He paused a moment. 'It's quite a show you're putting on.'

The lutist grinned.

'There's nothing like it, playing at the Festival. To be a part of it, to do our bit.' He looked a little out of it – Mike guessed he'd had a few himself, or the rush of playing was still in him.

'Well it's great. Everyone's enjoying themselves. I've never seen anyone play a lute before.'

'No? You should try it. It's very – very satisfying.' He blinked. 'You made it back this afternoon? Bike all up to scratch?'

'Yes, thank you.' Mike stopped and looked at the man. 'I didn't think I'd left my details with you earlier.'

'Sorry.' The man looked back in confusion. 'What do you mean?'

'You knew my name.' Mike looked at him. 'I didn't think I'd told you earlier.'

'Reece,' blurted the bike-man. 'I spoke to Reece. You're staying with him at Harvest House. Aren't you?'

'Yes.' Mike felt a stab of annoyance. He had liked the idea of just passing through places: a stranger, no story behind him.

'We're friends, Reece and I,' said the man. 'Us small businesses stick together.'

'So I've heard.' Mike looked around for Reece, but the fat man was nowhere to be seen. *Probably at the buffet,* thought Mike, and felt ashamed.

'I'm Simon,' continued the bike-man. 'And this...' he reached and beckoned his bandmates over. 'This is Matthew and Joanna. Matt, Joanna. This is Michael. He's staying with Reece this year.'

Matthew the drummer proffered a hand and Mike took it.

'Is he now?' Joanna took a sip of her drink and looked at him with cool blue eyes. 'How do you like the Festival, Mike?'

'It's ah – good. You guys; you're very good.'

'Thank you.' Joanna slipped past Simon to stand beside Mike. 'And how long have you been staying at Harvest House?'

'Only one night.' Mike found it both very easy to look into her eyes and very difficult to hold her gaze. 'I'm only passing through.'

'Then it's very good of you to come and see us. Thank you so much.' Her voice was slow and musical; a lovely voice. 'You're staying until closing time, of course.'

'I – I'm not sure.' Mike got to his feet. 'Sorry, I just – excuse me a minute.'

He left the bar and passed the buffet table, spotting Reece picking out cakes from a platter in the middle. He found the gents and squeezed through the narrow gap between the door and the hand-dryer that confronted him. He went to a basin and splashed water on his face, closing his eyes for a moment then opening them.

He looked in the mirror. Two urinals on the opposite wall stared back at him, and the cubicle door hung ajar. He was alone in here.

He ran his hands under the hot tap, scrubbing at them as if they were coated in shit. He rubbed his face till it was red. Then he stopped.

There were splashes of water on his shirt and jeans. His eyes were bloodshot from the soap. He could feel his brain blurring a little from the three tankards he'd finished.

He sighed into the mirror. He could feel an image wresting its way into his mind's eye; Joanna, the flute-player, with her cold blue eyes and scarlet lips. He exhaled again, locking eyes with himself in the polished glass. *Forget it. Forget her.*

He left the bathroom, holding the door for a ruddy-faced man hurrying in. He left by the front door without looking back. Outside, he nearly bumped into Reece.

'Ah, Mike. Glad I caught you.'

'Why?' Mike didn't apologise for sounding short with the big man. 'I mean – I was thinking of heading back.'

'Well, not just yet. I got you a pint.' Reece nodded over to the table beside him. A fresh tankard frothed, waiting for its owner.

Mike considered declining, then gave in.

'Cheers.' He hefted the cup in Reece's direction and took a swig. 'What is it, anyway?'

'Strange,' said Reece. He caught Mike's eye.

'It's made from grains and apples. Somewhere between beer and cider.'

'Sounds dangerous.'

'That's why they only make a few kegs a year.' Reece took a slurp of his own. The cakes Mike had seen him with were nowhere to be seen. 'I'm glad you made it tonight, Mike. It's good to have some new blood around.'

'It looks well attended. People are having a good time.'

'We do, we do. Every year, we hold the Festival. Every year we celebrate the end of the summer, the end of the harvest. It's a time of bounty and abundance.'

Reece was looking into the middle distance again. Mike drank a long draught of his pint, fighting his way towards the bottom.

'And what brought you here?' Reece returned to the present and looked at Mike.

'I'm just... passing through.'

'Well, I know that.' Reece's voice did not inflect much; his tone was flat, so that his words sounded neither accusatory or sarcastic. 'Where are you travelling to?'

Mike sighed.

'I'm not sure.'

Reece nodded.

'Then where did you come from?'

Mike paused for several long moments.

'My home,' he said, eventually. Reece nodded

again. And for a minute or so there was silence.

'I needed some space,' said Mike. Reece said nothing. Mike felt that compulsion again, to speak, to share. The big man seemed level-headed; even-tempered. And after tomorrow, he would never see him again.

'I did something,' continued Mike. 'Something I wish I hadn't done.'

Reece took a draught from his tankard and Mike followed suit. There were a few more people out here, sat at the tables or standing about. The drink gave Mike a lift, encouraged him to talk. No one else was listening.

'I slept with another woman,' he said. 'I – I cheated on my wife.'

There: it was done. It was told. Reece's face didn't change.

'Does she know?' he asked, and Mike felt a fortnight's worth of shame and regret boil in his guts.

'Yes,' he said. 'She knows.'

He thought of that night; saw flashes in his memory.

'We – me and Ellen – my wife and I – we were just having dinner. At home. On the sofa. Saturday night. And there was this knock on the door...'

He remembered that knock, remembered the carefree way he'd jogged to the door, opening it and feeling his innards plummet.

'I talked her down, got her to leave. We'd slept together once. *Once.* That's all it takes, isn't it?' Reece didn't reply. 'I closed the door and Ellen was there. She'd heard enough to know, I guess, but it still didn't hit her straight away.'

They'd gone back to the living room after the obligatory *Who was that? No one. Just work.* Picked up plates, cutlery, half-eaten dinners. Mike hadn't touched another mouthful. He didn't think Ellen had either.

'Who was she? Ellen asked me.' Mike looked around at the dark houses beneath the night sky. 'And that was all it took. All it took to make me spill. In that moment, I felt drunk. That's the only way I can describe it. You know when you feel drunk, and you just blurt out what's inside of you – when you don't want to hold it in your chest anymore. That's what I did. And I just...' He paused again. Reece didn't speak. 'I remember her face, first. It fell – when someone says their face fell, that's what it was. It turned from blank to, to ugly. Pale but blotchy as well. She cried, but she didn't sob. Just – tears, falling from her face. And her arms. She crossed her arms and held herself, as if she was cold, and rubbed her arms in her hands like she was trying to force warmth back into them. And I thought – I remember thinking – I've damaged her. I've damaged her inside.'

Mike stopped speaking for a long minute. Behind them in the pub, the clamour of the band started again, muted by the crowd inside. A gentle breeze sailed past and Mike felt it cold on his eyes where they had started to water.

'I left that night. Slept on a friend's floor. Went

back the next day and her car wasn't there, so I got a few things, stuck them in my bag. Took the bike and started to ride. I got a load of cash out – I didn't want Ellen to see my expenditures or where I was, I just wanted to be alone. Stupid, right? But it felt like what I needed to do. I called in to work, said I had some family emergency.'

Mike stopped again. He'd wondered if pouring his soul out would help ease the burden. It hadn't.

'The first night in a hotel I got in the shower and I stayed there for forty minutes. I couldn't wash it off. Wash her off. I felt like I stank of her, the one that I'd – well, of what we'd done. I still do. I wonder if I always will – if it's deeper than skin, if it will stay there forever.'

He touched his face. His cheeks were wet. He rubbed at them with his palms.

'Look, I'm sorry,' he said. 'I've poured that out on you. You didn't know what you were getting yourself into.'

'Have you heard from her?' Reece's voice was expressionless.

'She keeps calling. I don't pick up. She messages: I don't read them.'

'Why did you do it?' Reece took a sip from his tankard.

'I...' Mike had thought about it. Every night since leaving. Every night since he'd done it. 'I was weak. That's what they always say, isn't it? I understand it though. I was weak. I loved Ellen. I hate what I did. In the moment I felt like it would be okay; like I'd been hard done by and this was just balancing that out. Like it was my right. What a load of shit.' He let out a long, deep sigh. 'I fucked her over. I hurt us both. I've never regretted anything more in my life.'

Mike's throat felt dry, and he drank a draught of his pint. He didn't look at Reece, but he could hear his breathing, deep and laboured.

'So you've come a long way,' Reece said, and Mike looked up.

'Yes. Hundreds of miles, I guess. I don't know this area very well. I've never been here before.'

'You don't have friends out here? Nothing that made you want to come this way — nothing that drew you?'

'Nothing. Just a — a compulsion to leave. That she'd be better off without me.'

They fell silent again. Someone came out of the pub behind them and lit a cigarette. A man and woman in their early thirties — Mike's age — went back inside.

'Come on. Come back inside.' Reece nodded at the doorway.

'I think I'll head back, actually.'

'No.' Reece clasped Mike's shoulder, turning the movement into a pat. 'It'll do you good to have company. Better than stewing with your thoughts.'

Mike grimaced, divided.

'I'm heading to the bar,' continued Reece. 'Come in with me.'

He held the door open. After a beat, Mike

followed.

V

Mike let Reece settle him at the bar with another tankard of Strange. The band played on, fast, energetic, impassioned.

Confessing to Reece hadn't come with a rush of relief, but now he was back inside the pub, Mike felt like something had eased in him. He took the drink Reece passed over. His actions had haunted him since he'd left his home two weeks ago – cycling from them hadn't diminished them either. Confiding in someone for the first time had at least sorted the situation in his head – unpicked the tangled ball of knots that it had become. It had not helped his situation, but Mike felt he'd taken a step onto some sort of path. Some road that might – eventually – take him home.

The Strange tasted sweeter as the evening wore on. Mike felt more relaxed than he had done in a fortnight. For the first time since taking to his bike he wanted to forget about what he'd done, instead of mulling over it. Reece had been right.

He drunk a deep gulp of his pint. He could feel his feet tapping against the crossbar of his stool, his fingers rapping to the double-time beat. The crowd were still dancing. Someone had left the back door open so that occasional whips of cool breeze alleviated the sweat and beer musk of the place. He felt the urge to get up himself, and fought it down. He didn't want to make a fool of himself.

He watched the band. He could see the perspiration shining on their faces as they whirled through more music. Were they playing their own songs? Jamming? Or were they playing through some kind of folk standards? Mike knew nothing of the genre. But he was enjoying it. It sounded celebratory, joyous. It was just what he needed – just for one night.

The music rose to a crescendo – hands beat a tattoo on the drum, fingers vibrated against lute strings. Joanna's flushed cheeks swelled as she blew a final blast on her flute. Then the music stopped.

The crowd clapped and laughed and stomped. Mike joined in, beating the cups of his hands together. He heard Reece do the same at his side. The band downed their instruments and the congregation parted to admit them to the bar.

'Reece!' Simon wandered over, a pint in his left hand, taking Reece's meaty paw in his right. 'Good to see you, always a pleasure...'

Matthew, the drummer, caught the bar lady's attention immediately. Joanna came over to Mike.

'I thought you might have run away,' she said.

'I'm glad you didn't.'

'Just having a word with Reece outside.' Mike gulped at his pint. His buzz hadn't worn off. 'You sound great.'

'You weren't here to hear us.' Joanna took a sip from her own drink. It left a bright varnish on her lips. Mike couldn't help but notice the heave of her chest as she breathed heavily, warm from her performance.

'I caught the end,' Mike said. 'That's you done for the night, is it?'

'Not quite. One more set.' Joanna looked at him. Her eyes were wide and blue, so blue. 'You'll stay for that one, won't you?'

Mike looked at his watch. Ten o'clock. Where had the time gone?

'Yeah,' he said. 'Yeah, I reckon so.' He felt settled, comfortable. He felt some kind of... companionship? with the man he'd confided in outside, the man now nodding at the words of the bike-fixing lutist. Yes. Tonight, he was happy for the first time in two weeks. Hell, the first time he'd been happy in months. Years? Maybe.

'Good.' Joanna brought him back to the present. 'I think you'll like it.'

Mike caught her eye for a long moment. Inside, part of him twisted. He made to look away, but she spoke again.

'You're staying at Harvest House.'

Mike sighed.

'You're friends with Reece too.'

Joanna glanced at the fat man.

'We've met. But no. I saw you at the House.'

'Saw me?' Mike looked at her. 'At the House?'

'I'm staying there too. I saw you. In the garden.'

Mike felt something run through his body; something simultaneously cold and hot.

'You're staying at Reece's bed and breakfast?'

Joanna leant towards him. Was it intentional, the tilt of her breasts towards him? He looked away, fought the compulsion to look back, or splash water in his face, to wash himself.

'Yes.' They fell silent. The clamour of conversation, of thunking glasses, of clinking crockery surrounded them.

'Promise me you'll stay for the last set,' said Joanna, in her deep and musical voice. She retreated, straightening the folds of her dress, chastening herself. Mike felt the mix of compulsions, the desire to leave her, the desire to –

To what? He thought. *To what, exactly?* There something familiar about that feeling, something he'd felt with –

No. Ignore it. The feeling of... of...

What if she is *the one? What if he'd been wrong all those years, those years with Ellen? What if the one he was meant to be with, meant to love, was –*

'Yes.' Mike felt himself speak, as much to halt his thoughts as to provide a reply. 'I'll stay for your last set.'

'Thank you.' Joanna held his gaze, even as a

hand clapped on his shoulder. Mike turned, found Simon's face close to his. He recoiled slightly.

'Mike.' The lutist didn't seem sober. 'Mike. Play the lute with me. You said you would.'

'Wait. What —'

But Simon was pulling him, pulling him towards the band's corner. Mike fell into a stool, felt the bulbous instrument pushed into his hands.

'It's easy.' Simon's fingers twitched. 'Like a guitar. Only... upside down.'

Mike frowned. No one was watching. His fingers formed a shape on the strings, the easiest chord he could remember. E minor.

It sounded terrible.

'No, upside down.' Simon took the lute from him. Mike watched as his fingers made a shape, strummed out a wavering succession of notes. 'See? Easy.'

Mike made to take the instrument back. He could see what Simon was doing. But the older man was already immersed; plucking at the double strings, making some medieval-sounding melody.

'Sounds great.' Mike looked around. He forced his eyes from Joanna, from her red and orange-clad form, and saw Reece speaking to Matthew, the drummer. The chubby man was holding a flat cake and posting another into his mouth. Mike stood and made his way to the bar.

'Mike'll stay till closing,' said Reece. He and Matthew looked around.

'Sorry?' Mike edged his way into their conversation, turning away from Joanna.

'I said you'll stay till closing time,' repeated Reece. 'Of course you will.'

'Sure.' Mike glanced at Joanna. He could look, of course. There was nothing wrong with looking.

'It all stops at midnight,' said Reece. Mike turned around again, but Reece was talking to Matthew. 'He was asking about the circles today, you know.'

Mike frowned, and looked at them both.

They watch the circles.

Matthew nodded and looked at Mike.

'It's good to see you. Good to have fresh blood around.'

Fresh blood.

They watch the circles.

'Yeah. It's been a good night.'

He was drunk, he could feel it. This… Strange, it was strong stuff, and he'd chucked it down like it was lager.

'Mike.' He turned again. It was Joanna. 'It's nearly time. The final set. Help me prepare.'

She stood, and he followed.

'I can't play the flute,' he said. She laughed.

'Come with me.'

He trailed after her, out the open door at the rear of the pub. People stood around, people in various stages of blurring and double vision.

'What do you need me to do?'

He followed her to the bottom of the garden. There were few lights outside; he could only see by the light from the windows of the pub and the adjacent buildings. Beyond the low fence, the sea of wheat rolled and waved like a twilit, golden sea.

'Take this.'

Mike blinked. It was a tambourine. It was probably the same tambourine that had been strapped to the drummer's leg.

'And what do I –?'

'You'll know.' For a minute, Joanna's face seemed very close to his. He drank in the scent of her, floral and heady, like the scents of flowers and green, hallucinogenic herbs. He wanted to draw back, to refuse her, but he stayed still. 'You'll know,' she repeated, and moved to a spot in front of the fence.

Mike held the tambourine in his right hand. He stood close to Joanna, close because she was the only person he knew out here. He looked around; his vision was fuzzy with drink, with Strange brew. He looked up and saw the sky, the stars, the moon. The moon was papyrus-white, round but not quite a circle. Shit, he was drunk.

Joanna was looking at him; looking at him as if she was expecting something. He looked back, then looked at the tambourine in his hand. He shook it, once.

Shhk.

Yes. That was about right.

Shhk shhk. He found the rhythm of the thing,

the way his trembling hand turned into a low ringing, the slap of the ring against his leg forming a crack and clash; a backbeat.

Shhk. Shhk. Shhk-shkk.

Yes. That was it. That was it.

Shhk. Shhk. Shhk-shkk.

It was a steady rhythm, a strong rhythm, and he saw Joanna sway to it. He saw people around start to look at them, to watch them. He closed his eyes.

Shhk. Shhk. Shhk-shkk.

He wasn't a musician; wasn't a percussionist. But he'd made something, something rhythmic, a beat. People were watching; he couldn't bear that. But then he heard her, heard her voice.

He opened his eyes.

Joanna was singing. It was not a practiced voice, not a voice made for singing pop songs. But it rose above the crowd, strong and rich, and Mike saw the crowd from the pub start to gather in the garden.

Shhk. Shhk. Shhk-shkk.

Hold it. Hold that beat. That was all he needed to do. All he needed to do as that voice rose, high and lovely and commanding, into the night.

Shhk. Shhk. Shhk-shkk.

And her voice rose, though Mike couldn't distinguish the words that she sang. And as she sang, so the audience joined in. There were but a few words, and Mike could not make them out. But the crowd knew them, sang them, a refrain, a mantra. He remembered looking round at the field behind them, looking up at the moon above.

Shhk. Shhk. Shhk-shkk.

He was a component in this, a part of this. He kept his beat going, a simple beat, a primal beat. And as the voices faded, and her voice faded – Joanna's voice faded – so his beat faded, quiet at first, then quieter, quieter, until...

Shhk. Shhk. Shhk... Shhk.

*   *   *

Mike stepped out of the pub, out onto the road. He checked his watch: a little past midnight. To think he had been planning on hitting the road in the early morning. Ha. Well, he'd forget about that for now.

'Mike.' Joanna slipped in close to him and entwined an arm with his. It felt comfortable and warm, and he couldn't think of a way to shake her off without seeming rude.

'What were you singing back there?' he asked. His lips moved sluggishly with drink and his voice sounded thick and stupid, as if it were disconnected from the commands his brain was giving.

'One of the old songs.' Joanna leaned into him. She'd produced a worn denim jacket back at the pub and now she wore it unfastened, so that her dress of reds and oranges flamed inside the blue folds. 'Did you like it?'

'Yeah,' said Mike. 'I liked being part of it. It was

really...' he frowned. 'Good,' he said, finally.

'It's the first song of the harvest,' said Joanna. They passed the village shop. It was closed and its windows were as black and shiny as the pupils of her eyes. She began to hum, and Mike recognised the strains of the song she had performed in the garden, her back to the field. 'We sing it every year, every Festival...'

Mike blinked. He had thought of the field again, of the circles.

They watch the circles. Yes they did, and he wanted to watch the circles as well. He craned in his neck, trying to catch a glimpse of the enigmatic patches in the gaps between houses, barely illuminated in the moonlight –

And he tripped. His foot went down, clipped the kerb, dropped five inches further than he was expecting. It landed badly. He hopped and regained his balance – just.

'Shit,' he breathed. And then: 'Fuck...' His foot throbbed. He had forgotten the pain in the ankle till now; it had simmered down as the day went on and vanished from his consciousness along with the bite of autumn cold. He took a step on it and nearly toppled again. He was aware of Joanna, still hooked to his arm.

'Mike,' she whispered. 'Are you alright?'

He blinked again.

'Sorry,' he said. 'Hurt it... hurt it earlier. On my bike.' He remembered what the beak-nosed shop owner had said earlier: bikled, a mix of bike and cycled.

That made him a bikle-ist. Bike-list. He laughed out loud and Joanna laughed with him. She had a deep voice, he thought, deep and pleasurable to hear. Melodious. Her face fuzzed in his blurry vision, and he felt a little ill when he tried to focus on the white-gold strands of her hair.

'We should get you home,' she whispered. 'We need you fresh and well for tomorrow.'

'Hmm?' Mike leant on Joanna as she guided him back to Harvest House. She didn't object. 'You need me for what?'

'Mike.' She coiled an arm around his middle and Mike felt more of his weight settle into her. Her arm felt warm through the fabric of her jacket. 'You haven't been listening to a word I've been saying, have you?'

'Of course,' he said. 'Just, just tired. And... a little drunk, maybe.'

'Yes,' breathed Joanna. Her face was near his; her arms fast around him. 'Maybe.'

Neither spoke as they rounded the fulcrum of the village and approached the House. Mike was dimly aware of fumbling his keys from his pocket, dropping them even as Joanna knocked on the door and let them in. He discerned reaching the top of the stairs, trying too hard to get his key into the lock on his door. She'd helped him, a white hand on his own, and her face had been close to his, close as a kiss...

But he'd left her there, left the door to swing shut on its own as he lurched across the bedroom floor to the bathroom, just outrunning a burning bile that squirted up his throat and into the toilet bowl.

His eyes watered, and his stomach heaved again. He slumped to the floor, ready for another quake in his belly.

A cool breeze snaked in through the bedroom window. Outside, the ears of wheat waved and wriggled in a susurrus of collective movement.

VI

Mike slept fitfully.

He'd always been a poor drinker – he'd never got to the level of inebriation some of his mates had back at home simply because there came a point when his body raised a hand and said: nope. No more. Then he'd know he'd overstepped the line, and could only try to stave off the inevitable vomiting.

It damaged his sleep as well. True enough; a pint in the evening or a finger of whiskey before bed, those helped ease his passage into slumber. But any more than that and he was apt to wake in the night feeling hot, dry-mouthed and with the sensation of a warm, pulsing vice wrapped around his head.

And he'd certainly had more than a pint last evening.

The first time he woke was perhaps less than an hour after he'd closed his eyes on the spinning bathroom floor. Curtains closed: end of the show. That hadn't been sleep though, just respite from the apex of his sickness.

He'd pulled himself up from the tiled floor, cupped a hand under the cold tap, rinsed his mouth with it and spat the flecky water down the drain. He had repeated, then splashed water on his face and drank a few palmfuls. *Rehydrate.* Then he'd stumbled to the bedroom, hobbling on his re-sprained ankle, and fallen into bed.

He woke next when it was still dark. He was still hazy with drink, but he could recall waking up with a shout; a sleep-slurred plea for help. There'd been a dream again, another dream of running through... alleyways, he thought. Hedgerows? This time he had been aware of limping on his gammy foot (and as he remembered that, so his ankle flared in angry pain), limping *away* from something. And as he'd turned his head, in his dream, he'd seen orange and red and yellow, fire, as if he were being chased by the sun.

Come back, Michael. There's no escape that way. Come back. This is not your country –

And, in his dream, he'd forced himself awake, forced himself to escape.

Unlike upon his first awakening, the room had stopped spinning, and he needed water. He zig-zagged to the bathroom, his path of furniture and crumpled clothes barely lit by the moonlight drifting in through his window. Those curtains could stay open; light helped douse the remaining wobbliness in his eyes. He emptied a glass tumbler of his toothbrush and filled it from the tap. He downed it and poured another, making his way back to the bed. He paused by the window – the cool breeze was fresh on his oily skin. He jiggled at the handle; twisted and opened the window further, inviting in a good blast of fresh, wheaty air.

Then he fell back into bed, head pounding, and sunk back into sleep.

When he woke for the final time, the room was pink. A sunrise was casting a light through his window that, for the moment, was caught between red and yellow. This time, he felt no urge to get up and grab water. This time, he only wanted to drift back into a healing doze. But he couldn't. He was awake.

At least the breeze from the window was cool and refreshing. It smelt of yesterday's sun and today's blue skies. It was restorative, and Mike could feel himself drinking it in, the way his body drank in the cool sea on a hot day by the beach. But what was...?

He pulled himself up in bed. His head throbbed and his stomach churned, and he paused a moment till they'd settled. He could hear something, couldn't he? Something from outside?

The fresh air beckoned him forward and he reached the window. The light was already brightening, more gold than pink, and he squinted against the sky.

Below him, in the field, a dozen or so people were gathered. They were stood in the wheat, and Mike could see the long stalks came up to their chests and shoulders. They formed a ring, and at the centre of that ring...

They watch the circles.

The flattened patch, nearest Harvest House. It was empty and still, but the figures did not move from their positions around its circumference. It was as if they could see something there at the centre that he could not. There was a sound of singing on the air, but he could not see who was making it.

Although the morning was warm, warm for a September, he could see that all of them had pulled their hoods over their heads against the cold. He could determine from their bearings and hints of features that some were men and some were women. Some were taller than others, wider than others. Was this part of the harvest festival?

Bemused by the sight of the unmoving ring, but also curious, Mike stayed at the window. The other circle in the wheat, the one nearer the pub, was unmanned. Behind the horizon, the sun crept ever higher, till the base of it seemed to touch the field only by the outermost reaches of its halo. Mike stared down, and was struck by a thought – could they see him? Was he interrupting some little local ritual, important to the village folk?

Suddenly there was movement below. The figures did not move from their spots, but there came an animation over them, as if they had been standing to attention and were now at ease. Mike saw with a surge of panic that the figure opposite him looked straight up, straight at him. He averted his eyes quickly and moved from the window, wincing as he stepped too quickly on his ankle.

The eyes that had spotted him had been blue; cold blue. Mike was sure of it.

*   *   *

Mike could remember the previous night. What with his body's low tolerance to alcohol, he'd never suffered from those black patches that his mates claimed after a night on the lash. Last night was no exception. He remembered enjoying himself at the bar, remembered the lutist chattering at him as if they were best mates. He remembered getting out of the place, talking – talking to Reece...

That was something he wouldn't have done if he'd been sober. His glance flicked automatically to where his phone sat on the bedside table. A small white light flashed at the top like a little lighthouse beacon. He had messages waiting.

His stomach lurched.

Not now. Later. Maybe...

Later.

He remembered having a go on the lute for all of ten seconds. Remembered having a go with the tambourine – God, what a fool he must have looked. Jingling away in some pub garden with a folk singer. And everyone had been watching... He remembered the way she'd walked back with him, back to Harvest

House, with her arms all wrapped around him. She'd gone to kiss him, hadn't she? At the door to his room? It was hazy, that memory, clouded by room-spin and his bubbling belly. He groaned out loud and felt a shiver run down his body. He felt the urge to be sick again, limped, and spat a thick rope of saliva into the toilet. He stripped off the jeans he'd fallen asleep in, turned on the shower and dived into the boiling rain of it.

He scrubbed himself with his bare hands; hair, face, body. Soap lathered and splattered. He felt a thumbnail bite the skin between his chest and his armpit, and the cut stung with the shower gel. He didn't stop. He kept scrubbing, rubbing, washing away the touch of –

Who? Who this time?

Of the previous night. More bits of him stung: he hadn't cut his nails in his weeks on his bicycle. That felt good, like his washing, his disinfecting, was running under the skin, cleaning what it couldn't before. His eyes watered, tears washed away without pause by the hot, sluicing blast of the shower.

At last the water ran cold. Mike blinked and turned off the power. He stood for a minute, water dripping from nesting spots in the hairs of his body. He felt light-headed as he stepped from the bathtub; residual alcohol, heat. He rubbed himself down with the towel. When he was done he hung it back up. It was spotted with red. Not badly – pink, really, rather than red, just as if he'd padded his face with it after shaving, and his face was as big as his trunk.

His ankle was swollen, as if the spot in the crook between shin and foot had tried to inflate itself into a tennis ball. It had begun to discolour too, It was red for the moment, but it would soon darken to a blue bruise. Wonderful.

There were two ways to fight a hangover. Sleep it off, or power through it. Mike checked his watch. Eight o'clock. He would take the latter option.

He pulled on his clothes, discarding last night's shirt in favour of a cycling top. That would probably be fresher. He searched fruitlessly for the painkillers he'd bought from the village shop before giving up, pocketing his keys and heading out of his room.

The world had that hyper-realistic quality that comes with having alcohol in the bloodstream. He made his way down the stairs. His ankle throbbed and he winced with every step, but halfway down the stairs an incentive presented itself. Someone was making a fry-up.

He poked his head into the parlour area, opposite the reception room. The tables there were laid up with mats, cutlery and glasses. A coffee machine in the corner ejected a beautiful scent of roasted beans.

Mike wandered in and saw that the rear of the room backed onto the kitchen. There was a wide hatch in the wall and Mike could see a bald-headed figure working at a hob. The figure turned.

'Morning Mike.' Reece was chopping something below the level of the hatch. 'Made it down this morning then?'

'Just.' Mike grimaced. 'Coffee fair game, is it?'

'Help yourself.'

Mike found the black coffee button on the machine and a hot spray of caffeine jetted into the mug below.

'Full English, is it?' Reece asked through the hatch.

Mike's stomach flipped. Kill or cure.

'Please.' He lowered himself into a chair near the hatch. There was a jug of iced water on the table and he poured himself a glass, sipping it as his coffee cooled. The window offered a slim view; the House driveway and a slice of the high street at the end. No cars went past.

'No other guests for breakfast?' he called through the hatch. He still felt like the only resident in this house, despite Reece claiming he'd taken the final room.

'Already been down.' Hissing sounds gushed through the hatch.

'I suppose they didn't have so late a night.'

There was no reply.

Mike sipped his coffee. He'd always seen coffee and beer as polar opposites, and imagined the steaming coffee pouring into the cauldron of his stomach, scalding away the dregs of booze. He was feeling better already. As if to clip his enthusiasm, a glow of pain pulsed up his leg, like the soft red throb of a security alarm. The jury was out on if he could ride or not.

A door creaked behind him and Reece emerged with a plate. He ambled across the room, placing it atop a platter already waiting there on the table's placemat.

'Looks great,' said Mike. This had been the right choice.

'Enjoy,' said Reece, and left him to it.

The breakfast was filling, and it had the right amount of salt and grease to help settle his burning belly. Halfway through, he refilled his coffee mug, and the boost from it made him feel nearly human again.

He left his empty plate on the table and peered through the hatch for Reece. But the kitchen was empty. Shrugging, Mike left the parlour.

As he climbed the stairs, he had a sudden fear of meeting Joanna at the summit. He did not want to see her again. Not after last night. There had been something there. He'd felt a strong attraction to her, and he should have quashed it before he'd let himself be dragged along to the pub garden with her. He'd been drunk, but that didn't excuse it. He was a married man. He hadn't set out on this trip to hit on women, or even to flirt with them. Quite the opposite. He'd learned that lesson. Or he'd thought he had.

He unlocked his door and limped inside. He didn't have many possessions; it didn't take him long to pack. He pulled the sheets into something like a tidy position and left the room with its window open. Before going to the reception room, he wheeled his bike outside, conscious of the way he was leaning his weight on it. His foot was so swollen it had barely fitted in his trainer; now that it was in, it at least felt secure.

He returned to the front desk and rang the bell. Still no sight nor sound of another guest. Where were they? Mike had been awake from sunrise this morning; he'd heard no footsteps, creaks of activity or noise of any kind before he went to breakfast. And yet Reece maintained the other guests had all eaten. Had Joanna? Indeed, had it been Joanna's face that had raised to his own from the field this morning?

Reece squeezed into the room.

'Thanks for breakfast.' Mike held out his key. 'And for the room. I've had a lovely stay.'

'You're off, are you.' Reece's flat voice sanded away any inflection of enquiry from the question.

'I think so. I think it's time I headed... homewards.' Mike looked for a trace of acknowledgement in Reece's wide face, of approval perhaps, but there was none. 'Thanks again.'

'You can cycle on that leg, can you?' Reece nodded down to where Mike stood, one foot balanced stiffly on its ball.

'I'm sure I can push through.'

Reece looked at him.

'I'm sure the room will be free if you did change your mind,' he said.

'There's really no need.'

'But if gets too much. The nearest town after Dunkelton is a long ride away.'

'Thanks all the same.' Mike dropped the wheatsheaf and keys on the countertop. 'See you.'

He hobbled to the front door. As it banged shut, the knocker bounced just once with a final, tiny *clang*.

Mike wheeled the bike to the high street. He wanted to be out of Reece's view before he attempted to cycle. His foot felt like it was trapped in his trainer, like a victim in an iron maiden. But it would be fine. He would push through.

Push through.

He trundled the bike just around the corner, out of view of the Harvest House driveway. He looked at the high street. Turning right would take him to the main road, and right again would take him along that road, through the tree tunnel. Homeward bound. He thought of his mobile phone, zipped up in an internal pocket of his rucksack. He'd check it tonight. Perhaps he would even reply to a message.

He pointed the bike right and swung his bad foot over onto the pedal, leaving his healthy leg as the kickstand. He took a deep breath of fresh air, golden and rural and cleansing. Then he pushed away.

God, it hurt.

The roll of his ankle as he pedalled twisted whatever strings and ligaments were at the centre of the tennis ball his ankle had become. He let his right leg take the lion's share of effort, and felt the familiar pain of that unfair division. He pushed through it.

Houses passed on either side of the road.

There were no cars. He approached to the junction that spliced the village of Crookleton to the A-road, connecting it to civilisation. The globe of agony in his left foot pulsed. The channel of ache in his right leg smouldered. To the right, the road led uphill, gradually at first and then steeper as it climbed to the tree tunnel at its crown.

Mike put his foot down at the junction. A car passed on the main road, but there were none behind him. He went to put his foot back on the pedal, to pull away and start the ascent to the hilltop, then grounded it back onto the tarmac.

It was going to hurt.

Beyond the tree tunnel – had there been more hills? He couldn't remember fighting up any on his way here: that meant it was either level ground or he was going to hit the uphills today.

His heart sank. He didn't want to go that way. But he didn't want to follow the road to Dunkelton either.

His foot left the ground again... and plummeted back to earth.

Crookleton was composed of two streets, wasn't it? The high street with Harvest House and then the second street, with the Scythe and Stack. He hadn't followed that street through yet, but it did point in the rough direction that he intended to go. It must join up with a main road somewhere – and the village was all flat. With any luck the road would navigate around the hills – at least, it might stay flat until his blood was up and the cycling became easier.

He turned around and picked his foot off the road. The pain seemed to ease already, as if the tennis ball knew it was being indulged. He passed Harvest House, passed the MOT garage, concentrating on the freshness of the air in his lungs rather than the little agonies in his lower half. He kept his pace steady as he cycled by the village shop, but noticed he was pedalling quicker as he went past the pub – past memories of the previous night. He was expecting it to be closed, but its door was open and a couple of men outside watched him as he hummed past.

The houses on either side petered out and Mike found himself on a dusty track that led into the countryside. His fresh-pumped tyres were plump and his suspension equipped for this terrain; he'd bought his hardtail bike years ago instead of a flimsier road or hybrid model. After its service in Dunkelton there was no excuse not to give it a whirl on rougher ground.

The sides of this road were bordered by hedges and low fences. There were fields on all sides – circle-free, he couldn't help but notice. The track meandered gently, but seemed to be curving a little to the left. That was good. That was the direction of the A-road.

Mike's heart pumped faster; the country air filled his lungs. He perspired in the mild heat, sweating out the toxins that riddled his system. Already he felt better, felt as if he had made the right choice in turning off the road. He felt better about the previous evening too. If he looked at it in the right light, it seemed almost like a test. He had resisted Joanna, resisted her even as she'd followed him to his room and closed the distance between them. He hadn't succumbed. It did not right his previous wrong, and it was not an act of penance, but he was sure he had done right by himself.

A fly buzzed past in the warm air. There were few clouds in the sky; a good day for gliding. Mike looked up, but there were no paragliders overhead. He wondered where they landed; how long a walk it was back up to the launch pad up on the hill in Dunkelton. One day perhaps... *But not here*, he knew instinctively. He would not choose to come back to this strange village. Not again.

He'd been riding for half an hour or so. His right leg burned, but it felt good to be on the move. Even his left foot had numbed down to a dull ache. He hit a slight downhill gradient and let himself freewheel, legs on standby for a merciful few moments. Sun-baked dirt burst and spat under his tyres. He could see for a mile or so in front; there was a crossroads in the track, surrounded by trees. Would it have a signpost?

No. Mike paused when he reached the intersection. There were no signs, but the tracks perpendicular to his looked a bit more tyre-trodden, as if a greater amount of traffic chose this route through the countryside. Mike peered down the left arm, estimating the main road to be in that direction. If it was, it wasn't nearby, though Mike could see a few large buildings, barns, as if a farm was located over there.

Wait — what was that?

Mike's ears pricked up. It sounded like...

Traffic. Yes. He was close.

He strained his ears.

No — not cars. It wasn't the echoed rumble of nearby roads; it was a single engine. Mike peered down the track towards the farm. Something was coming his way.

His first thought was to ask for directions. Some native knowledge would steer him to the A-road and to civilisation. It was probably someone from the farm; they would know the quickest way out of the countryside.

Vroooooooom...

The chug of the engine was getting louder and Mike saw a vehicle turn a corner further down the road, onto his track. He felt a sudden and inexplicable urge to hide.

'What?' he said out loud, in answer to the unspoken thought. 'Why?'

But the urge did not fade, and as the engine grew louder Mike began to wheel his bike into the line of the trees that huddled around the crossroads. He knew it was stupid, knew what a fool he would look if anyone found him secreted under cover of the trees. And yet it was as if some other nameless sense had detected danger, and he felt it prudent to heed its warning.

He didn't crouch in the trees, only pulled the bike over their roots until he was surrounded by shadow. The track outside the trees glowed in the sun. He could hear the engine, louder now. It was big, growling. A van? There was a sputtering quality to its exertions, and he imagined a rusty old exhaust trembling and dripping as the wheels crunched on the rough ground.

A squeal of brakes, and a small truck passed by the trees. It slowed as it neared the crossroads, and Mike saw the bed of the truck was open and piled with timbers.

Just a farm truck, he thought, though he didn't speak out loud.

The truck stopped at the junction. Mike frowned. There couldn't be any other traffic to cause it to wait. What was going on? Dim, irrational fear grew in his belly like cracks spreading through ice.

Still, the truck sat. The engine growled and hacked, and Mike could smell the petrol creep into the verdant freshness of his hiding place. The cab was just out of sight behind the trees, but he could see the bed of the truck, trembling slightly as the engine rolled. He edged, half an inch at a time, behind the cover of the nearest trunk.

And then the engine coughed and the truck pulled forwards, turning right and climbing the hill that Mike had just flown down himself. He waited a further minute in the trees, till the sounds of the old vehicle had vanished, and rolled the bike out onto the track.

Stupid, he thought. 'Stupid,' he said out loud. His voice was small in the open terrain. *But no harm done.*

He took a sip of water from a bottle in his pack and climbed back on the bike, but whatever enjoyment he'd wrung out of the ride prior to stopping had dried up. His swollen ankle throbbed and his right leg objected to his demands with a twinge of pain. Mike grimaced and kept pedalling.

Push through it.

He passed the farm buildings. The ground around them looked churned up, but it had been hardened in the sun. Strange, stained steel equipment was bolted onto the sides of the barns and a few lower outbuildings; hoppers and chutes, things he wouldn't know how to use. He saw no people at the farm.

Beside the buildings was a field. Mike glanced in on his way past; a low fence with a stile at one end separated him from a herd of goats. One goat, bearded and horned, watched him with yellow eyes as he passed.

If another truck comes, a voice in Mike's head whispered, *will you hide again?*

He heard a sigh of reply from his own lips. He wasn't sure. But that last truck had been heading to Crookleton; there had been no turn-offs that he had seen on that road. He must be heading the right way now to get away from this village; towards the promise traffic and towns.

But how long would it take? It was a good job he'd made a start on the journey early. His ankle flamed; it felt as if the motion was injuring him more.

There was pushing through pain and there was ignoring something that hurt for good reason.

'Stop at the next town,' Mike promised himself. The words were whipped away by the wind, but speaking out loud helped to set the words in stone. 'Don't push your luck. Stop at the next town. Get a room, a Premier Inn or something. Have a decent meal. Sleep. Ride.' He growled as a flare of agony shot up his leg. 'Or get a train.'

The hills and fields undulated to either side. He had passed so many. He was heading uphill now; not enough to see the slope but enough to feel it. He looked at his watch – it was gone midday. He'd hoped to have hit the road by now – he'd imagined pausing at a shop somewhere for a quick snack and a drink around one o'clock. Well, there was still time.

He wondered how far he had ridden. On flat roads he probably would have gone twenty miles or more, but these tracks were a little harder to navigate and there was no way his legs were pumping at their maximum efficiency. Ten miles then? It wasn't a lot. Perhaps one of these small towns might have its own railway station – hell, even a bus stop.

'What now?'

Mike glanced down and around at the rear of his bike. There was a ticking sound coming from somewhere around the back wheel. It didn't sound serious, but it didn't sound healthy either. Must be a bit of grit or twig, caught in the chain. It would work its way out on its own.

He pushed further. This hill had gone on forever. He felt like he was climbing a mountain, helter-skeltering up and up without ever reaching the summit. But there — there the track terminated as it folded over and went downhill again. Mike pushed at the pedals, muscles filling with fire as he thought of the downhill stretch on the other side. He made it, grunting as the pain in his ankle reached an exquisite new level, and slowed his legs to a halt as gravity took over.

He could see a road, *fuck yes* he could see a road, a grey snake winding through golden brown fields and patches of trees. A couple of cars caught the sun as they crossed one another. Mike was heading straight down towards it. When he found a town, he might even treat himself to half an hour at a café. In fact, was that a cluster of buildings nearby? A village?

The ground shot by beneath him. Mike felt a smile spread on his face, a smile that turned into a grin. He kept his eyes on the bumpy track, but in his peripheral vision he saw birds fly overhead.

Free as a bird, he thought, and the notion pleased him so much that he said it out loud, throwing his words out onto the wind.

'Free as a bird!'

The ticking from his back wheel thrummed as the tyre span. Suddenly Mike frowned, and looked up again at the sky.

Not birds. Gliders.

They watch the circles.

Mike glanced to his left at the field that fell

away from his track, like a yellow carpet rolled down a staircase. A twist of surprise shot up his core.

Then the bike hit a dip in the track. It bounced; Mike clenched his fists around the brakes and jerked his eyes back to the path. Something cracked behind him. He felt the back of the bike drop and he held on fast, sticking out his right leg to regain his balance. It scraped through the dirt; cloud of dry dust billowed upwards. He ground to a halt, hopping off his bike and stumbling to the fence at the field's edge.

He panted, looked behind him at the bike. The rear wheel was still hooked on, but only by the chain. Something had become unscrewed; hitting the dip in the road had thrown the wheel off completely. But the broken bicycle was not at the forefront of Mike's mind.

The timbers of the fence were warm beneath his hands as he leaned his weight onto it. He looked down the slope, through the sea of wheat that waved in the sun. A town was lying at the bottom of that slope, a town that reached around the edge of the field in an L shape, so that it seemed to envelop it in a warm hug. In the field, a short distance from each axis of the village, were tramped-down circles of flattened crops.

'No.' Mike hissed the word before he had even realised he'd articulated it. 'It can't be.'

How far had he ridden? He couldn't have gone in a circle, could he? He'd turned left at the crossroads, followed the track...

The road before him was the one he'd rode in on two days before. He could see the tree tunnel nearby, just a right turn and a short uphill cycle away.

'Not after... not after all that...' he panted as the adrenalin started to leave his body, and dull disappointment and anger clouded in to replace it. Hours – he'd ridden for hours, on burning legs and a sprained ankle, only to emerge here, barely a mile from where he'd started. It was unfair; *fucking* unfair. If only he'd gone straight at those crossroads – would that have led him true? He cursed himself – then turned to look at his bike.

Hadn't he had it serviced just the day before? This shouldn't have happened. He thought of Simon, the lute-playing cyclist from Dunkelton. He'd seemed pretty out of it last night; maybe he was a drunk, an alkie. Fuck him. The bike had been fine. He'd broken something, or fitted something wrong. Now it was busted. What the hell was Mike meant to do now?

He looked up at the sky. The gliders were wheeling, turning back towards Dunkelton. They reminded Mike of vultures. *Free as a bird.* He snorted, and looked down again at the village of Crookleton.

There was activity in the field. A few figures were gathered in each circle; no more than half a dozen in each. He couldn't see what they were doing: walking around it, pointing at things. It didn't look ritualistic, like it had this morning, overseen from his window at Harvest House. It looked social, informal.

'Country bumpkins.' Mike spat over the fence. But only because the sight worried him, worried him in a way he couldn't explain. Something was proceeding, taking form down there. It troubled him. He turned his back on them and crouched down painfully by his bike.

It was something in the cassette; something must have sheared or fallen out. He could see the little wedding-cake of cogs on the ground nearby, and the chain was tangled in the spokes. He pulled the wheel free and grabbed what broken bits he could from the ground.

'For the love of...'

How was he meant to fix this? He wasn't a bike repairman – he only knew how to get on and pedal and occasionally change an inner tube. He'd only been riding the thing properly for two weeks! Maybe, sat in his garage with a cup of tea and a toolbox, he could have a crack at it, with some help from an internet tutorial. But out here, miles from anywhere? His options were ditch it or go back to the bike shop in Dunkelton. He didn't know which was worse.

He stared down at the wheat field. The stalks were tall: up to his chest. It was only the slope of the hill that gave him a view of what was going on at the bottom. Some kind of festival activity; it must be. Maybe they were all getting drunk in the field, all on that strange brew.

A phantom of his hangover manifested as a wave of nausea and Mike breathed in the sweet air, settling his belly. He would have to go down the hill. There was nowhere beyond the tree tunnel, not for miles. He couldn't hitch a ride, not with the remains of his bike under his arm, and he didn't want to just abandon the thing. He'd been through a lot with it over the past two weeks; it would be poor loyalty to leave it in a hedgerow now.

He fiddled with the wheel and chain. He could reattach the wheel to the frame. It would be unrideable – but it would be pushable.

He tightened the nuts as best he could, with dirt and oil-smeared fingers. He picked up all the broken pieces he could find and slipped them into a front pocket of his rucksack. He took off his helmet as well; no point wearing it if he wasn't riding. Then he wheeled the bike down to the road.

At least he hadn't landed on his sprained ankle.

The bike ran smoothly over the tarmac of the A-road. Mike leaned on it a little, trusting his weight to it as he limped. The pain was worse than it had been this morning. It needed rest; rest and ice. He needed to get home. But the road to Crookleton was pointed the wrong way.

The feeling of – what? Concern? Surely not fear? – rose in his guts as he neared the village. It was that same sensation he'd felt when the truck had passed him near the farm, that same warning propagated by that nameless inner sense. He wanted to be hidden, unnoticed.

Sure enough, as the road lowered, it dipped below the level of the field, and he could not see what was going on in there amongst the wheat. That meant he was out of sight too. He could see the occasional roof surfacing over the crops, but little more. Not even a church spire provided a beacon. Had he even seen a church in Crookleton? He couldn't remember one. What kind of isolated village didn't have a church?

He reached the junction onto the high street and paused for a long moment, as he had done that morning. There was no traffic to be seen. He fought the feeling of instinctive danger that battled his common sense – *just frustration*, he argued, *just frustration at coming back, anxiety at needing to leave* – and started to wheel his bike down the high street.

He crossed the road and reached a bus shelter. The timetable was old and sun-bleached, and he didn't recognise the name or logo of the bus company. He squinted at the chart. Was that... He checked his watch. It was an hour away. He would have to wait an hour for a bus to Dunkelton – and then however long for a bus to a larger town. He wished he'd just caught one this morning.

The sun was still bright, the air still warm. It was unseasonable; a late summer. It beat waiting here in the cold and rain, at least.

Mike checked his watch again. He was a doer, not a sitter. How far was it to Dunkelton? Five miles? He could walk it and be there no later than the bus would arrive.

An angry flare from his ankle. Perhaps not.

But would the bus come at all? The timetable was ancient; what if he waited all afternoon for a bus that had long since dropped Crookleton from its route? No, there must be something coming. It was a Saturday afternoon; someone in the village must want to pop out of town for a drink or something to eat.

He propped the bike against the side of the shelter and slid himself down onto the hard plastic seat.

Rest the foot. Wait for the bus.

VII

It was quiet in the village of Crookleton. No cars passed the bus shelter on the high street. Occasional birdcalls twittered in the nearby gardens. *But the strangest thing*, thought Mike, *is that there are no people.*

There were only a few houses at this end of the high street and they were large, detached piles. But Mike hadn't seen a single person enter or leave any of them. The houses thickened as the street went on; it was possible that there had been some villagers knocking around there while he sat with his back turned. But the sense of emptiness was worrying. He strained his ears for the sound of a bus. It had been fifty minutes.

There might have been no people to see, but Mike felt sure he could hear some kind of activity happening somewhere. He realised that it must be the figures he'd seen in the field on his way down the hill.

Every now and then he heard a raised voice carried on the wind, and a thumping as of tools put to use. Whatever they were doing, it must be pretty important – not one of them had returned to their home in the midst of it.

Another five minutes inched by.

The sunlight was beginning to fail. Mike glanced around again at the houses. Whereas an hour ago the windows had been turned to black mirrors by the direct sun, now he could see the vague shapes of furniture inside the houses. It was voyeuristic, and Mike felt a perverse amusement as he squinted in at the houses. Maybe he'd be able to catch a bit of telly in someone's lounge; *Countdown* or something.

A movement caught his eye; a curtain trembled in a first-floor window. Mike averted his eyes as if caught in the act of spying, then peeked back.

All was still.

A cat? Or had someone been watching him? If so, why would they?

Mike shivered. His clothes were still a little sweat-damp from his cycling and he felt a chill steal across his body. Now that the seed was sown, he could not shake the feeling of being watched. Had it been so all afternoon? Had unseen eyes stared down at him, shielded from view by the glare of the sun?

He checked his watch again. The bus was five minutes late. He felt anxiety start to rise and he quenched it. It would come. There was probably a flock of sheep crossing the road; something like that, delaying it. Mike smirked.

Five minutes more. The sun was dipping lower in the sky. Twilight wouldn't fall for many hours yet, and the weather was still warm; warm enough for a barbeque, or a for a few beers out in the garden. Then why was his skin prickling as if a cold wind was trickling past?

Mike checked the faded timetable again. Sunday... Monday to Friday... Saturday. He ran a finger down the column and grunted. It should be here. It should have *been* here, been and gone. What the fuck was holding it up?

The festival, thought Mike. *There are no cars here, so no buses either. The service is cancelled for the day.* And as soon as he thought of it, he knew it must be true. Maybe it wasn't cancelled; maybe the bus company just knew that no one would be leaving the village or trying to reach it this day. But he knew in his heart that there was no bus coming.

What choices did that leave him? He could walk to Dunkelton; get a bus from there. It was Saturday and they would run till late. Then he could get a train back to the city. Only... how far was it to Dunkelton? Five miles or more? Could he manage it on his sprained foot?

He'd thought not earlier, but what were his other options? Grab a lift, he supposed, if anyone in the village was inclined to give him one. Did Reece have a car? Surely; this was the twenty-first century. He'd seen one parked around the side of the House.

Besides, he didn't know anyone else to ask. Apart from...

Joanna. She was spending the night at Harvest House. How far had she travelled to reach here? She must have driven.

No. That wasn't worth considering. He did not want to see Joanna again.

Mike fidgeted on the uncomfortable seat and glanced behind him. There was no movement from any of the houses. For a moment he considered a third option:

Spend the night at Harvest House. Rest your foot. Get to Dunkelton early; as early as possible. Get the first ride out of there. Mike smiled suddenly. *Glide if you have to.*

His smile faded. He did not want to spend another night here. There was something about Crookleton that disquieted him. The festival; it all came back to the festival. Mike felt simultaneously as if he was being treated as an outsider, an intruder at their celebration, and an integral part of it. It wasn't right that Joanna had made him a player in her performance last night; this wasn't his festival and he could not sympathise with it. It was some isolated rural tradition he did not understand and did not wish to.

Besides, his last two nights had left him ill, injured and acting out of character. He thought again of how he had confessed all to Reece. Why had he done that? He'd heard of beers getting drinkers lairy, up for a fight, and yes, getting confessional. But Mike hadn't intended to divulge anything of his faithlessness to anybody. Even now, the temporary relief he'd felt had dissipated, and he wished he'd kept his story to himself. He'd had enough of Crookleton, and musing over his stay only helped reinforce his decision to leave.

Mike stood. His legs had seized up; he should've kept them moving, even if just to drum on the pavement. His ankle throbbed – well, he'd had plenty of time to get used to that. He leaned on his handlebars and started to walk.

He reached the junction and turned left. The hills arced away to either side of the road and he remembered his cycle there yesterday had been all uphill.

It had been a long day. How many miles had he ridden before walking now? All on hurting legs too. Mike thought of his own bed, of collapsing back into that soft blanket and sleeping the sleep of the dead. He'd be hurting in the morning, oh yes, but he wouldn't have to get up, wouldn't have to haul himself onto his bike and ride for another day. He could just lay there, drinking in sleep like water...

And for the first time in two weeks, he imagined Ellen lying there beside him. Of waking before she did, turning himself softly in the bed to look at her and laying a hand on her sleeping body as it rose and fell with her breathing. He wanted that, he knew. He wanted that more than anything else in the world. He wanted to go back to her – and for her to let him.

The sound of a car grew behind him till it overtook, curving out into the middle of the road. Its speed compared to his laboured walking made Mike groan. He looked behind him – the junction to Crookleton was still in sight. This was going to take a while.

He battled on. He thought of his bed when his pain flared; thought of his wife to keep him going. He'd get there – he'd be home tomorrow night, by hook or by crook. Dunkelton – bus – train – home. Home.

Another car passed, this one going the other way. It wasn't going to Crookleton: Mike knew it for sure, as if by instinct. There were no barriers around that village, no guards controlling which people might enter or leave, but no one was visiting Crookleton tonight. No one apart from those who were *meant* to be there – Joanna and Reece and the festival-goers. Mike wasn't meant to be there. He would be long gone by sundown.

The junction behind him had slipped behind a hill or a corner. Crookleton had vanished from sight. Mike felt a surge of satisfaction. He was making progress, gaining ground.

It was darker than it should've been at this time in the afternoon. The low sun was obscured by the surrounding hills so that the road took on a cloudy colour, though there were no clouds in the sky. Still, the light would be good for another two hours at least. More than enough time to reach the town.

Mike glanced backwards again. The road felt like a kind of purgatory; a line between two fixed points. He could not see the place he was travelling from or to; he could be anywhere on that line, with no way of measuring his progress till the first signs of life appeared ahead.

His ankle was hurting again. He'd make it to Dunkelton; of course he would. He had no other choice. But he hoped he wasn't doing any lasting damage to his foot by pushing it so.

The sound of a car grew behind him. Mike edged to the side of the road to give it room to overtake. He smiled to himself. Before he'd got the bike out a fortnight ago, he'd cursed cyclists when he'd encountered them on the road. They held up traffic; they were a hazard to motorists. Now his point of view had switched. He wasn't doing any harm on his bike; hell, he was doing less than all the fume-squirting vehicles on the road. If anything, he had more right than them to use the roads. It wasn't like he didn't pay road tax.

He heard the car behind him slow down and wondered if the driver was complaining to a passenger about him.

Mike frowned. The car still hadn't passed him. He was about to turn around when the engine *vroomed* and a truck – not a car – swooped around him and parked at the side of the road, hazard lights flashing. Mike stopped short. He recognised that truck.

For a moment he stood still. The truck's exhaust coughed and dripped water onto the road, just as he'd imagined earlier. But now the bed was empty of cargo. As he watched, the driver's-side door clunked and opened.

It was Reece.

One trunk-like leg planted itself on the road, followed by the other. Reece heaved his chunky frame out of the cab and nodded.

'Mike. Fancy seeing you here.'

'Reece.' Mike shifted his weight and winced as his ankle glowed red. 'Is that – is that your truck?'

Reece looked at the vehicle as if surprised to have stepped out of it.

'No.' He stepped away, as if to distance himself from it. 'Borrowed it for the drive. To Dunkelton.'

'You're not going to the festival?' Mike remembered the trust he'd invested in Reece the previous night – and the chill that had stolen over him when he'd hidden from the truck that morning.

'I've got to pick something up,' said Reece. He jerked his head towards the town ahead of them. 'Do you fancy a ride?'

Mike eyed the truck. The engine was still on, and it growled.

'No thanks,' he said, after a long pause. 'I think I'll take the fresh air.'

They stood for a minute.

'You're sure?' Reece made no move to return to the truck. 'There's room for the bike in the back. Why aren't you riding it?'

'Think something shook loose earlier.' Mike looked down at the bike, then back at Reece. 'Think I took a wrong turning earlier. I thought I'd be miles away by now.'

'Yes, you said you were moving on. Now you're headed to Dunkelton.'

'I'll get a bus from there. Start on my way home.'

Reece's bottom lip jutted in thought, and he glanced down at his watch.

'You'll have to get a move on,' he said. 'Last bus is in half an hour.'

'You're joking.' Mike stepped forward, wheeling the bike with him. 'On a Saturday?'

'Yep.' The flat expression on Reece's face didn't change. 'Reduced service for six months now. What can you do.'

Mike glared at the road ahead.

'There's nothing else? Nothing leaving Dunkelton? It's not even the evening. How does anyone get anywhere around here?'

Reece shrugged.

'Well, I'm driving. You're welcome to join me. You've another four miles to walk otherwise.'

Mike's stomach sank. What choice did he have?

He looked once more at the truck. It was just that; just a truck. Nothing to be wary of. Reece was the closest thing to a friend he'd had since leaving home. He was being helpful.

'Okay.' Mike took another step forward. 'Thanks.'

'No problem.' Reece beckoned in the direction of Mike's bike. 'Let's get this on the back.' He wrested the bike in his meaty hands and lugged it into the bed of the truck. 'Go ahead,' he said, nodding at the passenger door, and leant to strap down the bike.

Mike walked – limped – to the cab, and clunked open the door. He settled himself on the seat. It smelled strange in the cab, like wet dog and farmyards. Reece climbed into the driver's side.

'Right. Let's go.'

He flicked on his indicator, and waited an excessive amount of time before pulling out and setting off down the road.

The truck was loud and rattley. The smell of animal was thick in the air, contained by the smeared windows.

'Whose truck did you borrow then?' Mike looked across the cab. Reece was driving slowly; thirty miles an hour in a sixty zone.

'Bloke across the road. Has a bit of farm land.' Well, that explained the smell. Maybe the farmer friend had carried a sheep in here. Reece switched up to fourth gear; Mike looked forward expectantly but the truck only crept up to thirty-five. 'You going to get the bike fixed?'

Mike thought of Simon's bike shop.

'I think I'll leave it till I get home.'

Reece nodded. 'Could be for the best. No point getting it sorted just yet.'

'I suppose not.'

Fences and hedges crawled past on either side.

'I'm not sure where the bus station is in

Dunkelton,' said Mike. 'Would you mind pointing me in that direction when we arrive?'

'Sure thing.' Reece rested a thick arm on the window frame, and dug out a clear bottle from a compartment between the two seats. 'Water? You look parched.'

'Cheers.' Mike took the proffered bottle, and began to fiddle with the label.

'You got lost then? Cycling out of Crookleton?' Reece prompted.

'Yes. I just wound up back on this road. Went in one big circle.'

'It happens a lot round here,' said Reece. 'All the tracks curve around till you're facing back the way you came. Without you even noticing.'

'I expect it's obvious when you see it from above. Like those gliders do. I expect it's all...' He trailed off as something in his brain seemed to connect. It was like a memory triggered by a snatch of a pop song; too brief to recall, but in there somewhere to stumble on later. 'All circles,' he finished quietly.

The cab was humid and bouncy, and Mike felt his stomach begin to protest again. He hadn't kept hydrated today: he knew that. He twisted the cap off the water bottle and had a swig. It tasted odd.

'I always keep water around in case of emergencies,' said Reece, as if reading his mind. His eyes didn't leave the road ahead. 'It could have been in here a while.' A car rushed up behind them and overtook the battered truck.

'I thought this wasn't your truck?'

Mike looked at the fat man, but there was no reply. Suddenly, his stomach felt very fragile.

'I think you might need to stop,' said Mike. 'I think... I think I need some fresh air.' His mouth was salivating, his stomach knotting. He blinked hard and tried to ignore the jolting of the truck. It was no good. He was going to be sick.

'Please,' he hissed. 'Pull over a moment. I need...'

The truck was slowing, but Mike's vision was blurring. He scrabbled for the door handle, wrenching it open before the truck had completely stopped. He felt his stomach twist as he lurched from the cab, and he bent double as burning vomit bubbled up from his throat. His aching stomach hurt and he stumbled back. Behind him, the truck door slammed.

He fell back against the truck. He could feel himself sliding down the side into a heap on the floor and made to push himself up and away from it. His legs failed. He fell to his knees and pain exploded somewhere in his foot. A shadow fell over him, but his eyes were too watery, too blurry to make out the features on Reece's face. The fat man was saying something, but the signals weren't transmitting; his brain couldn't make sense of it.

A blackness crept in from all sides and Mike felt himself fall face down on the ground. He couldn't discern the moment when he passed into unconsciousness.

VIII

The waking world was dizzy and nauseating. Mike's eyes were shut – or was the world all dark? He could see nothing, had no idea where he was. He could feel something soft beneath him. He remembered cycling, and waiting for a bus, and circles – something about circles. Had that been real? The memories were fragments, like those in a dream. Was he waking after a night of drinking at the Scythe and Stack?

His eyes were open; shapes were dim around him. This wasn't his room.

The memories were resolving, braiding into sensible strings.

He remembered walking to Dunkelton. He'd met Reece. Got into his truck...

And then...

Where was he?

The room spun as he rolled onto his side. He had gone to pull himself upright, but his hands hadn't worked. Now he felt that they were tied together, fastened behind his back. A shiver ran through his body. He was scared.

He fixed his eyes on some shadowy patch in front of him, anchoring himself as the room continued to sway and pitch. He needed to keep calm, keep calm and find out what was going on.

He looked around slowly. He was on a bed – he was sure of that. The dark forms around him must be furniture. This wasn't a prison cell, or a dungeon. It was a bedroom, and there was a window set into the wall nearest the bed. He could see pale lines of light at the edges of the curtains; a rectilinear halo. He would get to the window and find out where he was.

Wait a minute. Before he did that – what could he hear? Voices – he was sure of it. Not individual voices, as of a conversation in an adjacent room, but a whole crowd of voices, whispering somewhere nearby. *A legion*, he thought, wildly. Just outside his room.

He blinked, hard, and took a deep breath. *It's never a bad time for a deep breath*, he'd been told once. He filled his lungs to bursting point and breathed out, feeling the oxygen spread through his body. As it dissipated, the fear returned.

No. Whatever was happening here, he couldn't afford hysteria. He had to swallow down that terror, keep calm.

His legs hadn't been tied. He rolled them and pulled himself to the edge of the bed. The world spun again and his stomach lurched. For a moment he thought he was going to be sick again. But the feeling passed, and he sighed with relief. He could feel the hurt in the muscles of his belly; they'd been worked a lot in the past couple of days.

He stood, easing himself off the bed. He tottered, fighting a fuzzy head and badly sprained ankle without any arms to balance himself, and managed to remain upright. The window was only three feet away, and he reached it with a heavy limp.

His hands were tied wrist to wrist, crossing over each other in an X shape. Mike kept going to use them and feeling the bond stop him, and rather than open the curtains he was forced to nose his head through to see the outside world. He leant his forehead against the cool glass.

The bedroom looked out over the field. The sky was clear and the moon was huge and yellow, illuminating the village below. He could see the expanse of wheat trembling in the breeze, and the buildings that bordered the field. Over to the right the line of buildings was centred by a larger mass, easily identifiable by the light of a bonfire near its grounds – the Scythe and Stack. Mike recognised the view; he knew where he was. He might be incarcerated in a different room, but he had been brought back to Harvest House.

The window misted with his breath and he was forced to rub the condensation away with his hair, headbutting the window and wiping from side to side. He might have felt ridiculous, but the sense of danger was too overpowering. He edged back from the glass to avoid blocking his view again.

There was movement in the field below and Mike looked down to where he knew the circle lay. It was empty no longer. Some kind of construct had been erected there, something built of timbers and ropes. It was perhaps seven feet tall, drawing over the level of the wheat that surrounded it, and had no particular shape that Mike could recognise. If pushed, he might have said it looked like a child's climbing frame.

There were people in the field too. Mike could see their heads and shoulders, hooded as they had appeared that morning, standing around the perimeter of the circle. As before, they did not move, but Mike could see activity elsewhere: a few people were below him in the garden of the House, and he could see more silhouettes passing near the fire by the pub. He could hear voices; not whispers but quiet, reverent conversations going on in the garden. On the other side of the field, he could hear the sound of music; drums. A trickle of sweat cooled on his temple in the breeze from the cracked-open window.

There was a knocking sound from below, followed a few moments later by a slam. Someone had entered the house. Mike pulled his head back from the curtains, losing himself once more in the darkness of the room. He fumbled, blind, unsure whether to break for the door before anyone made their way upstairs or to hide somewhere in the room.

He could hear footsteps on the stairs. Gloomy

vision was returning to him, all shades of black. A light clicked on in the landing outside and a slit of yellow appeared at the base of the door. A key scraped in the lock. The door opened.

Mike held his breath and stood still.

A man walked into the room. He wasn't robed like the watchers in the field; he was dressed in smart jeans and a chequered shirt.

'Michael?' His voice was familiar, but it wasn't friendly. 'You awake yet?'

Mike remained still. He wasn't hidden – not by a long stretch – but he was stood in the shadow between the wall and a wardrobe. If his visitor stepped into the room, towards the bed... he might be able to run for it.

'It's nearly time,' said the figure, and he stepped further into the room, beyond the halo of light cast by the open door. Mike shifted his weight, readying himself to run – and the floor creaked in reply.

The figure turned to face the corner. Mike recognised him: Simon from the bike shop, Simon the lute-player.

'You *are* awake.' Simon came forward.

Mike launched himself. If he could catch his captor off-guard, shove past him, he stood a chance of escape. But the smaller man caught him, taking Mike's momentum in his shoulder and wrapping a firm arm around him. The sudden stop sent bolts of agony up from Mike's ankle and he grunted out loud.

'Not so fast.' Simon's voice was mild, resigned.

'All over soon, don't you worry. It's about time for you to come downstairs.'

'Why?' Mike grunted again as Simon turned him, by his arm. 'What the fuck is going on?'

'Only the Festival.' Simon gave his arm a short tug, and Mike had no balance to resist. He let himself be walked out the door and across the landing.

'Why do you need me?' Mike blinked in the light. 'What did... did you drug me?'

'Not a drug,' said Simon. They reached the stairs, and Simon prodded him, encouraging him to descend. Mike's head hurt and his body felt spent. 'Just a mixture. A potion.'

'A what...' Mike's voice trailed away. Whatever he'd been sucked into, it wasn't sane. What did these people think they were? Pagans? Druids? A fresh fear rattled through his core. How could he reason with anyone who thought like that? What was this Festival?

Simon opened the front door and led Mike out of Harvest House.

The night felt clean and empty. It was warm, as uncannily warm as the day that had preceded it. He felt no chill as Simon led him off the door step and closed the door behind them, hard enough for the iron knocker to bounce once with a metallic clang. He could hear the murmur of voices more clearly now, and the beat of a drum in the distance. Was that Matthew, Simon's mate from the previous night? Was Joanna with him, or was she out there standing in the field, up to her neck in wheat crops? Simon started to lead him round the side of the House.

'Don't take me there.'

Mike heard a voice and realised it was his own. He didn't sound as scared as he felt.

'Don't take me round there. Just... let me go.'

Simon stopped and looked at him. Mike's voice, acting without any consciousness, continued.

'I don't know what it is you're doing. I don't care what it is. But I don't need to be part of it, whatever it is. I was only passing through. I didn't mean to be here, to interrupt anything. But I'll go now. Just... let go of me. I'll find a way home.'

Simon looked at him for a minute more. Then he started to walk again, pushing Mike along with him.

'Fuck you then.' Mike looked behind him. He couldn't run, not with his sprain and his hands tied. But he couldn't go along with this, whatever it was. He had to move when he had the chance.

They rounded the side of the House. The gate to the garden was open; the murmur of voices carried through from beyond. Mike felt like a criminal being escorted by a policeman; a limping, broken prisoner being walked to the scaffold. His heart jumped at the image and he remembered the timber construct in the field. It couldn't come to that, could it? It wouldn't be that?

Faces turned to him as Simon led him through the garden. Some of the crowd stopped their conversations at their entrance and some continued, as if his presence was only mildly diverting. Their nonchalance terrified him. Whatever they were doing with him, it was *normal* to them. Expected. They weren't even dressed as if for a midnight ritual – they wore smart if casual clothes like Simon. This wasn't so much a ceremony as an evening out.

Mike looked around as they worked their way towards the field. The bonfire was out of direct sight, but the flickering glow was visible above the sea of wheat. His surroundings were lit by the light of the moon, turning the garden to shades of black and bone. Deep shadows pooled where the moonlight couldn't reach; shadows that could hide a man from sight.

He blinked and looked up at the moon. It was full, yellow.

A Harvest Moon, thought Mike. *A circle in the sky.*

They reached the bottom of the garden and a woman opened a gate in the low fence. Her face was turned away from the moonlight, but Mike caught a glimpse of a beak-like nose. The shopkeeper or the bar lady? He didn't know. Simon shoved him through the gate and into the field.

Even through his mounting fear, Mike felt a strange sensation as he stood at the boundary of the field, in the sun-baked mud that bordered the crops. It was something like trespass, and for a moment he felt like a child, caught in the act of being somewhere he shouldn't be, about to be reprimanded and thrown back to the wrath of his parents or worse. A sense of expectation filled him, and for a moment Mike thought it was something internal, something unique to him.

An ingrained anticipation of some punishment for this infraction. But then he realised it was something in the air, something like the pressure that builds up before a storm. A densness in the atmosphere, as if all its molecules could electrify at once and light up the sky.

He could see the top of the strange construct poking above the ears of wheat. The ropes were not part of its construction, he saw – they were some sort of pulley system, or winch. Some sort of farming machine? A primitive combine harvester? His thoughts were truncated as Simon pulled him to a halt.

Mike looked around. He realised that the ring of hooded figures around the circle had gone; he could see nobody in the field. There was only Simon at his side and the crowd of people in the garden behind him. He noticed the crowd had fallen silent and, a moment later, he felt Simon unknot his wrists.

Run! a voice in his head screamed, so hard that his feet twitched and his body swayed to do so. Yet something kept him rooted to the spot; the sure knowledge he would be caught, yes, but something more. A kind of obscene fascination. He looked around. Somewhere in the silence, something bleated.

The wheat rustled and Joanna stepped out from the wall of stalks. Had she been crouching to remain hidden in there? Mike did not believe so. Somehow, he understood that she had been there since the moment he had stepped into the field, only protected from his view by whatever force was there in the field with them. She wore a full-length black robe, the hood pulled over her head. He could see the waves of Teutonic blonde hair flowing over her shoulder blades and saw with a start that she must be naked beneath the gown, for triangles of skin, pale as the moon, glowed behind its ebony folds.

She paused before Mike, and he saw that Simon had retreated whilst he had stared at Joanna. Dimly, he realised he had missed his chance to flee. Joanna looked Mike up and down for a minute. One of her hands held something inside her cloak, the other was pressed to her breast. She wetted her lips and fixed her blue eyes on his.

'Come,' she said, as if commanding something that went on all fours, something kept on a collar and leash. Mike felt himself stumble towards her, as if any other course was inevitable. She turned, and led him into the wheat.

It was like stepping into another world, a world of heady harvest scents and tickling grains. He heard rustlings around him; not just of his own movement or Joanna's but of something else, something circling them outside of his vision. He couldn't tell if it was something physical, stalking them from the field, or some trick of the wind. If it was the robed figures from the circle, they would surely catch him if he ran.

His steps were faltering and damaged. They led him to the circle and Mike saw that it was neither raw earth or cut crops after all, but carefully flattened wheat, as if a colossal rolling pin had gently and carefully bent the stalks down in an anti-clockwise direction about the centre. The whole circle was perhaps thirty feet in diameter. Joanna's feet were bare and they padded nimbly over the bed of stalks.

Mike looked up at the squat machine in the centre of the ring, and saw it for what it was. The construct was a pyramid of timbers and spars, centred over a hole dug into the ground. A crane. Ropes hung from the apex of the pulley system, dripping into the opening in the ground below. That hole... It was sheer, rectangular, seven foot by three. It looked like a grave. He could not tell if there was anything in the pit.

Sounds came from the fields around them. Mike's head twisted, trying to turn and alert him of any danger, but it was too dark to discern anything in detail. Strange shapes seemed to surface from the high carpet of wheat; pointy shapes like raised branches, and Mike saw they had formed an outer circle around the space he and Joanna were in. His heart beat hard in his throat, as if he were trying to swallow a tough pulsating fruit. Another bleating came from somewhere nearby, louder than the last.

'Midnight approaches,' said Joanna. Her rich voice was not raised, but it carried about the field, as if conducted by that static sensation that filled the air. Mike saw a change in the surrounding shapes, a new erectness, as if they were now standing to attention.

The figures from earlier, he thought.

Joanna pulled her hood back and pale hair fell down the back of her gown. Her other hand remained hidden. She reached out, slowly, as to beckon at someone outside the circle, and the robe slipped away from her shoulder, revealing a moon-brightened swell of breast. Her complete lack of self-consciousness made the situation more unreal, more terrifying.

A rustling in the stalks grew louder and a moment later a low shape burst through the wheat. Mike looked at it fearfully. It was a goat, horned and bearded, led by no leash or tether. Its belly was full and fat. He had no idea if it was young or old, male or female, but it seemed large to him — if it approached him, it would come up to higher than his waist. He would have thought the ambience of fear and strangeness would disturb the creature, make it dangerous, but the goat was calm and made no attempt to approach him. Its mouth was settled in that strange animal manner that appears like a human smile. It followed the promise of Joanna's outstretched hand, and when it was close to her she knelt before it.

He heard her whisper. The goat stared ahead dumbly, blinking its odd, square-pupiled eyes, even as she reached up into the loose hair and skin of its neck and stroked it. Mike was unable to look away. The scene was so alien to him: the woman and the beast, beauty and bestiality. He found himself wishing that the goat would buck, kicking its sharp hooves into the woman before it. Surely the circle around them would not stand by; surely they would rush to her aid and give him the chance to run, to lose himself in the rows of wheat that surrounded them like a sea. He knew where to run. Harvest House was behind him, the bonfire by the Scythe and Stack was to his right. He would run to the left, towards the road. Burst through the hedge and fence hollering and waving his arms at any passing car. Even if he looked like a madman, it would get him away from this strange place. They had already drugged him, kidnapped him – where would it end?

His thoughts of escape were cut short. As he watched, Joanna knelt up to the goat's face and pressed her lips to its mouth. Mike felt his own jaw drop and his stomach roll. She held the kiss, her eyes closed, lit by the eyes of the goat that stared into her face. Mike was revolted. He imagined her lips pressed to the flesh of its smiling lips – grinning lips – finding the shape of its blunt yellow teeth behind them. After several long moments, Joanna pulled back. She stood up and held out her arm.

'Come,' she said again, but this time Mike's feet were planted to the ground. He shook his head, his disgust lending him fresh fortitude. Joanna placed a hand over the goat's neck and walked with it towards him. Mike wanted to step back but remained still, transfixed, nightmare-like. His eyes were on the goat, on its devilish eyes and its upturned lips. In his peripheral vision he saw movement; the figures in the field drawing closer.

'Come, Mike.'

Joanna held out her hand but Mike ignored it. He had to run; he had to escape. Whatever happened, even if he was caught straight away, he needed to get away from this place. He heard the swishing of stalks behind him and turned his head a little. Two figures were behind him, two masked figures. One face was covered with a wooden visor, carved in the likeness of leaves. The other face was only half covered, its mask shielding its eyes and topped with thin branches that raised the man's height an extra foot. Mike recognised the frame of the branch-masked figure. It was Reece. Both the figures were holding long sticks; after tearing his eyes from their masks, Mike realised the sticks were scythes. Reece turned his scythe a little in his hand and its blade caught the moonlight, turning silver.

Mike swallowed and looked back at Joanna. She did not smile, did not frown, only beckoned him once again. The goat bleated quietly at her side.

Mike stepped forward.

They walked to the wide crane that straddled the grave-like hole in the ground. Joanna stepped through the timbers, drawing the goat along at her side. Mike heard the approach of the scythemen behind him and stumbled after her. On the other side of the crane, two more robed figures advanced, one with a crescent shaped mask and the other with a diadem of brambles and thorns.

Joanna turned back so that she was facing Mike with Harvest House behind him.

'The summer is over,' she announced. 'And the harvest is ripe.' The goat bleated again, a little louder now. No sounds came from those people nearby, nor from those gathered in the garden of Harvest House. 'Let us give thanks for the Harvest, and for the sun, as we sow now for the season of the moon.'

There was quiet. Only the whisper of the wheat crop and the odd bleats of the goat floated up into the air.

The two figures on the far side of the crane stepped forward and pulled at ropes. Mike watched as the cords that hung down into the pit began to slither upwards, over the top spar of the crane. A leathery shape at the end of the ropes was revealed. Joanna pulled it towards her, and unwrapped the shape. It was a cradle, and she knelt to wrap it around the swollen body of the goat.

'The offering is prepared.'

She stood and looked at Mike. The goat began to fidget uncomfortably, crunching its hooves and breaking the wheat stalks on the ground. Joanna took a step away from the animal, drawing her bare feet away from the danger of being stamped on.

'Approach,' she said. Mike did not move for a moment, but a soft stamp from behind reminded him of the scythes at his back, and he limped forward. Joanna opened her robe as he drew closer, and he saw the full globe of her breast, punctuated with a large, dark nipple. She withdrew something shiny from the gown and held it out to him.

A knife.

Behind her, the goat bleated, and Mike watched as it began to float. No, not float – it was being raised, raised by the crane around them. The ropes and timbers creaked in the still air. It bleated again, and again, its panic rising with its body.

'Take it,' said Joanna, the knife in her raised hands. It was long, a foot from the point of its blade to the base of its handle, and curved like some specialist butcher's tool. Mike did not take it.

'I can't,' he said. 'I won't do it.'

Joanna did not move. The knife stayed proffered between them.

'You must,' she said. 'It is the hour between dusk and dawn; the hinge between sunset and the break of day. We must give thanks for the harvest.'

Mike looked at the knife. He couldn't kill a creature, not like this. But the knife was a weapon, freely offered.

Joanna locked eyes with him, as if reading his mind.

'You cannot hurt us,' she said. 'Not tonight.'

The goat cried out. It was fully suspended now, cradled over the maw of the pit, but within reach of an arm – or a knife.

Mike reached out and took the dagger from Joanna. He felt something like a static shock as he wrapped his hand around it and held it like a lifeline.

'Why?' he asked, forming the words around the fist-sized heart in his throat. 'Why must I?'

'Thanks must be given. Life for life.' Joanna stepped back, giving him access to the squirming creature over the pit, but Mike stepped forwards, closing the gap between them. There was a sound from behind him; the smaller of the two robed scythemen stepped around him, blocking him from Joanna.

'The offering,' called Joanna, and Mike saw the two blades of the scythes swoop closer to his face. A threat.

He could not win this fight. If he turned to attack them, they would kill him. He was sure of it. The long scythes would cut his throat before he got near enough to land a blow. He turned to the goat.

It was only an animal.

A living animal, he thought. *A living, terrified creature.*

He took a step forward.

Animals are killed all the time, he told himself. *The world over.*

Suddenly, the thought of every animal he'd ever killed came to him. Fish he'd caught and finished off with a hammer. A pheasant on the road, spinning away from his car in a spray of blood. Slugs frothing as they died a melting, salty death in the garden.

Do it, he thought. *Do it to save yourself.*

The goat cried, hooves pedalling in the air. It didn't look devilish anymore; it looked pitiable. It square eyes bulged in its tufted face.

A waste of life, thought Mike. *It's one thing to kill for food, or by accident. Another to kill for... for...this.* He looked around. These people must know it was pointless. This sacrifice would not work, would not please any non-existent gods. This life was being cut short for nothing.

Mike felt a cold, hard object touch the back of

his neck. It was not sharp, not the bladed side of the scythe, but he took its meaning.

Then make its death mean something to you, he thought. The notion seemed absurd, but he clung to it. *Don't let it die in vain. Do this and live your life freely, to the full.*

He stepped to the edge of the pit. How deep did it go? Its bottom was shadowed. It might descend to the centre of the earth. Hanging above it, the goat's face was less than two feet from his own. He could smell the thing, like a wet dog and farmyards, smell its fear. He braced himself on his good leg. He raised the knife. He paused.

'I'm sorry,' he whispered. *Sorry you have to die for this. For them. Sorry you have to die to save me.*

He held the creature by the top of its neck, turned it on its ropes. It began to scream, as if it knew what was coming, as if his own dread were transferring into it.

Do it. Do it. End its terror. Do it. Do it –

He reached around the goat's throat and pressed the knife to it. He yanked it around, fast, hard, and yelled out himself as he felt the blade push through skin and muscle and cartilage and bone, and kept pushing, needing to do this now, not wanting to leave the thing half dead, suffering more than it had to. He realised he'd closed his eyes but did not dare open them. The goat was bucking, screaming, gurgling, and he felt it kick him square in the chest. He stumbled, jerked open his eyes and came face to face with the poor creature. He scrambled and grabbed for the ropes that held it in suspension, steadying himself. The goat's eyes were terrified but dimming; it was dying. Mike pulled himself back, disgusted with himself. His hands were hot and sticky and red; he'd dropped the knife without realising it.

The goat wheezed out red bubbles from the clumsy gash in its throat. Pink foam sputtered from its smiling lips, lips that Joanna had kissed. Its legs kicked sporadically, sending it swinging on its ropes. After a minute, Mike knew it was dead.

He felt wretched, revolted. And relieved. It was done. This awful horror show was done.

He stepped back from the pit, limping on his injured foot. He stumbled and caught himself on the timbers around him, feeling the wood slip under his bloody palm. Already, the goat was being lowered, the ropes that held it creaking over the timbers of the crane.

Joanna came to him. Her eyes were fixed on his, but her voice resounded throughout the field.

'The sacrifice is made. The offering is buried like the summer sun. We welcome now the season of the moon.' She turned to the west, to the Scythe and Stack and the bonfire that glowed over the wheat sea. 'Follow me,' she said to Mike.

He did so, trailing after her over the furrowed ground, wading a path through the golden stalks. He could smell the blood on him, like copper and salt and meat. More than anything he wanted to wash, to clean it from his skin in a scalding shower of water, to burn away his guilt.

A cloud passed overhead, masking the moon for a moment with a thin veil. A surge of excitement swelled in Mike's chest: could such a moment of darkness allow him to escape? Or did he need to? The thing was done; their sacrifice was made. Perhaps all that was left was a celebration feast, a commemoration of a sacrifice successfully made?

'What now?' he said. He saw Joanna had heard him: her head cocked to one side as she walked. Above them, the cloud cleared, and the moonlight shone down unhindered.

'Your part is nearly over,' she replied.

'My part.' Mike's pace was slow and painful and, as if aware of his flagging momentum, Joanna slowed as well. 'What is my part? Why are you using me?'

'It could not be one of the villagers.' Joanna looked back at him. Her face was monochrome in the night, but he could still see the arctic blue of her eyes. 'That would be no worthy sacrifice.'

'You can't believe it matters,' grunted Mike. He paused, the pain in his ankle too much. 'Any of this. It isn't… it doesn't work. You made me kill that animal for no reason.'

Joanna stopped too, and turned around.

'Of course there was a reason,' she said. 'Just as the sun sets and the moon rises, so the dead return to the earth to rise again. As the fields grow, they are fed on sunlight and rain, they are cut and their seed returned to the earth to grow once more. As above, so below. These are the rhythms of the earth and the sky, the sun and moon, the night and day. So we learn to live by the cycle, to prosper with nature, to survive with it and to live on.'

'It's not necessary.' Mike shut his eyes as the pain and the fear rose. When he opened them, Joanna had closed the gap between them. She stood only three feet away. 'All you're saying. Nothing changes what happens here. We live, we die, we make... we make mistakes along the way. And when we're dead there are more people left to do the same thing. You don't need this... all of this... to make that happen.'

Joanna stared at him.

'I do,' she said, at last. 'We do.'

She began to walk again.

Mike remained still. He kept seeing the goat's terrified face flash in his vision, the terrified eyes bulging as its torn throat spat and spurted and gaped. Its blood was congealing on his hands and it felt disrespectful to wipe them on his clothes as if it were muck or grime. He grabbed handfuls of the wheat around him and let it soak what it could from his palms. The goat was only an animal; he knew this. But it had died for him, for his survival. When he got away from here, he would go home. He would go to Ellen. He would be alive, and he wouldn't waste that life.

Then he started to limp, surprising himself by following in Joanna's wake. Like it or not, he was part of this now. When it was over, he would get as far away from the village as he could.

The ground was bumpy with clumps of hard dirt, and the wheat crop hid stones and uneven furrows. Mike wondered how Joanna could stride so confidently over the rough terrain with only her bare feet. He had to be cautious as he stumbled on, limping on his sprained ankle.

The pain had intensified since he'd been marched into the field by Simon, and he thought perhaps the potion he'd been given had initially numbed it. He'd certainly felt out of it as he'd first followed Joanna into the circle, as if his head was fuzzy with too many tablets. But the clean air had helped to clear his head, and fear and adrenalin had sharpened his senses.

The ordeal with the goat made him to feel his sprained ankle in a new light too. It was trivial compared the feel of the scythe on the back of his neck, the dagger in his hand, the kick of the goat as it bled to death. It was something he could push through. He almost felt confident as he followed Joanna towards the second circle.

There were sounds ahead. While the first circle had been quiet and sombre, the second was alive with the crackling of logs and the spit of flames, the irregular pulse of drums and a low chorus of voices. Mike did not know what awaited him, but imagined a repeat of the previous night: the pub filled with food and merriment as the bonfire lit the dark sky. He even managed a smile – perhaps there would be an orgy. That would put his prior misdemeanour in perspective.

Joanna pushed through the wheat into the circle, and for a moment she was framed by the flames as a silhouette of deepest, darkest black. Mike stepped into the ring and felt the heat of the fire. This close to the blaze, everything was lit in oranges and yellows, and the shadows pooled in voids of complete darkness.

They rounded the fire and Mike saw the Scythe and Stack behind it. Its garden was lit with flame torches and he could see people milling about, popping in and out of the pub. He had no doubt they would be eating, drinking. It looked harmless, rustic and traditional – but Mike knew better now. This community was tethered to something older, a repellent tradition that should have been left to die in the past. If he was left to join the revelers, he would sneak away unnoticed, leave this bizarre place behind him.

Joanna led him into the garden. People looked at him, but none seemed horrified or even surprised at his blood-soaked hands and clothes. They knew what had occurred in the first circle. Perhaps they felt lucky they were watching this final episode of the night. They did acknowledge Joanna however; nodding their heads, bowing slightly, as if she were some authoritarian figure to be shown respect.

She's not one of them, thought Mike. *She's only visiting. She's staying at Harvest House, the same as me.* Who was she? Some kind of itinerant priestess? Another thought occurred to him. *How many more villages has she visited?* How many times a year did this happen? He would be glad to get away and, when he did, he would call the police. This kind of thing couldn't happen. There was no excuse for it in this day and age.

A man he didn't recognise offered him a tankard, but Mike waved him away. The man scarpered. Now that he felt awake and alert, it wouldn't do to compromise his senses. He knew that the worst was over: that with the sacrifice made, the trials of the night were done. But the villagers had kidnapped him, drugged him. He couldn't let his guard drop.

Joanna had moved away to talk to someone closer to the pub. Her eyes flicked back to him constantly, as if she knew his thoughts were straying to escape. For his part, Mike stood amongst the clusters of drinkers, edging gradually away from them, disguising his movements as limps on his ankle.

If the chance came, where could he go? He was on foot – not that there was any way of taking a car or vehicle out of here – but the main road was still his best chance of getting away. Even if he had to stagger for a few miles till morning, till cars started showing up, he would be moving away from Crookleton. Or would the villagers chase him? Bring him back? How important was he to them?

Even if he did make it to the road, even if he did evade the villagers till morning, what would he look like? Covered in blood, no wallet or phone... He would look like a madman, a killer. No one would pick him up. Except perhaps the police... but then he would be calling the police anyway...

He looked at Joanna as his thoughts tumbled in circles. She had turned away, tightened her robe across her body. She wasn't looking at him.

Mike sidled away, towards the gap between the pub and the adjacent houses. He could hide somewhere in the village, couldn't he? It seemed stupid, demeaning even, but he could creep away and hide behind a garden wall or fence until morning. Then he could make his way to the road and to civilisation. It was easy to chase down an injured man; harder to find one who was lying low.

There was no one in the alley between the buildings. If he could get down there, perhaps hop the fence to avoid anyone outside the pub, he would be free to find a hiding place. Somewhere far enough away to avoid immediate detection, but close enough that it wouldn't tax his injured foot...

'Mike. Come with me.' Joanna was there at his side. He shot a longing glance at the shadows of his planned escape route.

'Why?' Had she noticed what he was doing? He thought so.

'Your part is not yet finished.'

She laced an arm through his and he was conscious of the thin veil of fabric separating her body from his own. She led him towards the field.

'What is it now?' Mike glanced behind him. People were leaving the pub, milling into its garden.

'We have one more task to perform before the hour is done,' said Joanna. Mike saw that there were people, people in robes and masks, standing around the bonfire. 'Then you will be free of this place.'

'Why me?' Mike began to slow, reluctant to continue. Joanna's words unnerved him: what was he expected to kill this time? 'And why not just invite me here? Why take me prisoner like this? I'm not part of it.'

'You wouldn't stay of your own accord.' Joanna looked across at him. 'You tried to leave. You wouldn't stay – not even to have me.' She tossed her hair and pulled on his arm. Mike stumbled after her.

'What you're doing isn't right,' he said. But she did not turn again.

They reached the fire, and the ring of figures surrounding it parted to let them in before closing again. The figures all carried scythes, the tools of the harvest, and their false carved faces flickered with fire and shadow. They were close to the flames; Mike felt uncomfortable with the heat. Everything outside the ring was pitch-black by contrast.

He followed Joanna around the blaze, and saw the bonfire was not, as he had assumed, a conical construction. On this side, he saw it was a crescent, a moon shape. It reminded him of the shape of the scythes that surrounded him, that had so recently been held against him. It towered up, just beyond the height of his head, glowing like a molten mountain. The space in the middle, the alcove in the centre of the crescent, was little more than three feet wide, walled on three sides by fire. Embers hissed and kindling cracked.

Joanna held his hand and they turned, backs to the blaze. The harvest moon hung above them. Mike noticed that some of the masked figures had marched around the bonfire, so that half a dozen of them were positioned from the points of the crescent shape, as if to block him and Joanna in.

His pulse began to quicken and his stomach started to boil. A drip of sweat ran down his temple that had little to do with the heat of the fire.

'We have given thanks for the Harvest and sown the seeds for the coming year,' said Joanna. The figures around them did not move, but all faced her. Mike could not see outside the circle, the orange blaze was too great, but he imagined her rich voice was carried to the garden and to the group that congregated there. He would not be surprised if her words traversed the breadth of the field, borne on the electrified air. Joanna continued.

'So ends the season of the sun. Already, the moon rises to take its throne for the winter.' All faces bent upwards towards the moon. Mike's foot twitched. His body was poised; some primeval instinct, his inner sense, was reacting to a danger that his mind had not yet fully computed. Before he could commit to sprinting, the figures (*his guards?*) looked down again, and his moment was gone.

'We welcome the moon.' Joanna paused a moment, her eyes closed. Mike heard a whisper, as if all the figures nearby had murmured a response. The speaker opened her eyes. 'As we bury the sun, so we give fire to the moon, that it may light us with fortune and prosperity till the turn of the season.'

She turned to Mike.

'It is time,' she said.

The figures stepped forwards, tightening their arc around Joanna and Mike. Their blades glowed orange in the flames. Mike backed away, cringing back from the heat as he was forced towards the centre of the blaze.

'No,' he said. Then, as the danger dawned on him, he shouted: 'No! NO!'

His heart rate doubled, tripled; he began to hyperventilate. A hot, throbbing sensation burned through his face, filling his ears with a *thump-thump-thump* of blood and blurring his vision. His stomach flipped and his skin felt suddenly cold as his blood rushed to fill his limbs and brain.

The figures stepped forwards again, hemming him in. Joanna retreated, slipping between their cloaks. Their masks were demonic in the firelight; animal, inhuman, monstrous.

The air seemed thick; sludgy. Mike felt as if everything were moving in slow motion, like in a nightmare before the reprieve of wakefulness. He was conscious of his own body, the systems inside it that pumped blood and air, that hauled muscles against bones to give him movement. The heat from the fire around him seemed to be inside him instead of out, filling him up before it singed his skin, turned it to crackling.

Then this was death: a kind of dreamlike hyper-reality. He wondered whether the pain would be rendered in that exquisite clarity, or whether his body would shut down, save him the torture of feeling his meats roasting and his fats popping, his fluids hissing and vaporising in the flames. It was unbearable; the sensation of absolute, impending agony.

He had to run. Even falling on the blade of a scythe would be preferable to the fire. Even if they caught him, threw him back into the blaze, he had to try.

His feet moved slowly in the baking air. He felt every muscle in his body move as he bent to sprint at the guards before him. Were they experiencing this same, torturous clarity; this life in slow-motion? Or was he really moving this ponderously? Could they read his every move; plan for his freedom run and move to block him?

Did it matter? He had no other choice.

Mike ran. He launched himself forward on his right foot, throwing himself out of the enclosure of the bonfire. He remembered tales of people in deadly experiences gaining extra strength from the proximity of certain death. Would it be the same for him? Would his frantic thrashings be enough to force his way through the line of figures?

The masked guards were expecting his run. They raised their scythes, barring the crooked handles across their chests, ready to block him, to shove him back.

It was Mike's injured ankle that saved him. As it hit the ground for the second time, some knot of dirt or submerged stone threw him off-balance. A fork of agony crackled up his leg and he fell, diving forwards as if flying into a rugby tackle. He crashed between two of the figures, beneath the wall of scythe-shafts raised to stop him and, before he had even realised he'd landed, Mike was scrabbling forwards, grabbing at handfuls of wheat and heaving himself up onto his feet.

Behind him there was confusion; cloaks spinning, scythes clattering. Mike did not turn to watch. He only ran; at first in an arbitrary straight line directly away from the fire, then bending his limping steps to the left as he headed in the direction of the main road.

He heard shouts behind him; the muffled crushing of crops as they gave chase. The agony returned to his leg and he stifled a scream that was composed of as much hysteria as pain. He couldn't run much more; couldn't push any more on his ankle. He felt his leg buckle and took a chance – he threw himself to the ground.

The smell of dirt, dry and earthy, filled his nose. The crops were musty, grassy.

Had they seen? Had they seen him dive to the floor? Were they approaching him now, ready to haul him up by the scruff of his neck and return him to the fire? Mike couldn't bear it. He thrust his face to the ground, clamped his hands over his head, shrank himself into the rooty earth.

He heard rustles, choked footsteps. Some further away, some closer, as if his pursuers had fanned out to find him. There were no steps heading straight for him.

Below the sounds of the chase and his own pounding heartbeat, Mike could hear nothing. Nobody spoke, no new calls or directives were communicated across the field. The search was executed in silence. Mike kept his own breathing quiet, each tug of air shallow and filled with the taste of ground. One rustling sound was getting louder, coming closer to him; they hadn't seen him, he thought, but he was still in danger of being tripped over.

He peered up. The long stalks reared over his head. The stars were bright in the sky above. Behind him, the faint glow of the bonfire was visible.

The padding of footsteps on dry earth got louder, the *swish* of an approaching body.

Mike tensed, readying his leg to push himself up and away. There was adrenalin, or at least the absence of pain, in his aching muscles. Should he run if discovered, or should he charge at whoever it was that found him? Would he have more chance running or attacking?

Part of him – a strong part – desired the latter. He imagined wrestling away the scythe, battering his assailant with the shaft and breaking for freedom. He thought of the scythe blades dancing in the orange bonfire glow. How far would he go to escape? Would he kill?

He remembered the heat of the blaze as they'd trapped him in the crescent-shaped fire. They would have killed him. They still intended to kill him. He would do what he had to.

He thought of Joanna. Was she amongst the searchers?

The rustling nearby paused. Mike placed his palms to the floor, ready to spring. Whoever it was, they were somewhere to his left. Whether he attacked or ran, he would have to twist and then jump. He took deep breaths, readied himself.

The rustling began again, but the footsteps were moving further away. Mike breathed out. They hadn't found him.

He looked around. Wheat pressed in all around. It would be his cover; his shield. He worked himself up onto his knees, quietly. He was well below the cover of the crops. He began to crawl, padding his way forwards on hands still spattered with the goat's blood.

He stayed alert, ears straining for sounds. His heart thumped and his breath panted. The crops brushed and bent and he paused, scared that his own movements had been as loud and obvious as those of his pursuers. It felt as if he were making a racket, drowning out everything else. But there was nothing – no sounds of anyone close by.

How long was the field? A quarter of a mile?

Half? Mike knew without sticking his head above the surface of the wheat it would be more like the latter. He wouldn't cut a straight route; his progress would be slow and painful.

The need to escape at least alleviated something of the horror of his situation. By concentrating solely on his escape, he blocked the full scope of the threat behind him. He clung to hope by moving a foot at a time, of inching his way to freedom, always thinking of the path ahead, the slow crawling path. Fragments of thoughts flared in his head – *fire, burning, sacrifice, death* – but they did not germinate into thoughts. Better to ignore them. Best to get away from them.

He crawled on.

Small stones pricked the tight skin over his kneecaps and he felt the dust and dirt cake his face and arms. He tried not to set the stalks around him shaking too hard in case they would be noticed, waving like flags in the night, but his haste was getting the better of him. He paused for a moment, listening for any sounds of approach, and when he began again he did so slower than before.

Perhaps they've given up, he thought, but knew it would not be so. It wasn't about the ritual anymore – it was about capturing him, keeping him quiet. They must know that if he were to escape he would call the authorities down on them; finish their antiquated ring of black magic. Maybe his pursuers had relocated to the edges of the field – perhaps they were waiting for the first glimpse of him to emerge before pouncing on him.

Mike's heart sank. If they were there waiting, would they kill him on the spot? Slit his throat just like he had killed that goat? Or would they subdue him, drag him back to the fire? The stakes were high now. Mike did not know what they would do, but he did not stop moving. He would cross that bridge when he came to it. One thing at a time; one inch at a time. He had to reach the edge of the field.

He stopped still.

He'd heard something, something nearby. It had stopped now, and he had only heard it slightly, over the sound of his own movement. He remained dead still, frozen by survival instinct. Could it have been one of them? A figure, masked and armed, ready to reap?

The noise did not repeat. It had been an animal, scuttling sound, as if some fox or creature had brushed its way through the wheat. Perhaps that was all it had been. And yet, why would it stop, as if it knew it had been heard? Why could he no longer hear it? Another thought occurred to Mike. He had seen no animals in the field at all, besides the goat he had killed. No mice or insects nesting in the crops, no birds or bats flying overhead. It was like that energy, that sense of static and charge about the field, deflected any form of wildlife.

He waited another minute in still silence. After hearing nothing more, he started to move again.

He had no idea where he was; whether he was deep in the field or near its borders. He could not gauge his distance travelled; time seemed to have both flown and crawled, and he did not know how much ground he'd gained on his hands and knees. Maybe he would be crawling till morning – when light would reveal his whereabouts, but bring with it the hope of rescue. Perhaps –

A scuffling noise, close by, and a dark shape exploded through the wheat and barrelled into him. In the split second before it hit he thought it was an animal, some black big cat, but it pinned him to the floor and he knew it was human; human and female.

Joanna's attack had knocked him onto his back and she straddled him now, using her weight to keep him still and holding his wrists down with pale fingers. He rolled and bucked beneath her, forced a hand free and pushed at her, shoving her away. Her face was flushed and she panted, dark tongue licking at her teeth as she fought him. Her gown had fallen away from her shoulders, pooling round her hips, and her body was white in the moonlight. Her nipples stood out, hard as bullets, and her hair fell into his face, whipping him with dirt and wheat dust.

They scrabbled in the silence. The only sounds were their breathing, quick, shallow, gulps of air, and the muffled crumpling of the crops around them. Mike fought the urge to call for help; it would only summon the others. He reached for her throat, a soft spot, a weakness. She let go of his other wrist and gripped him by the chest. He felt nails pull at his skin a moment before she clawed at his face, scraping for his eyes and leaving red streaks of pain down his cheek.

His hand found her neck and he dug a thumb into the hollow of her throat. He pushed hard but she shook him away and rammed a hand under his chin, smacking his head back into the ground and holding it there. He saw her reach down with her other hand, down into the folds of her robe, and grabbed for her wrist.

His body was hurting, expiring. It had been beaten and battered, drugged and damaged. Now he could feel Joanna's will to defeat him overtaking his own drive to survive.

There was a flash of moonlight from the black folds of the robe and Mike struggled to hold back the pale hand that now held a long knife. It was already bloodied; stained on the handle and blade. *Goat's blood.*

The sight of the weapon lent him a surge of energy. He forced his back against the ground, forcing his hips up and into the fork of her legs, lifting her away from him, like some perverse inversion of sex. She gnashed her teeth as she lost balance, and he bucked and threw a hand up in a wild punch that landed under her throat. He heard her choke and felt her fall back.

He breathed out, gasping for air, dimly aware that he'd pushed up on his legs and that the sprain in his ankle had been pushed over some precipice of agony. And then a hot, metallic, numbing pain shot up his other leg. He groaned and twisted and looked down to see Joanna. At first he thought she was holding him by the leg, gripping him by the calf, then he realised her fist was tight around the knife handle. The blade was somewhere in his leg.

His mouth dropped at the surreal sight and the shock blocked some of the excruciation he was sure should be overwhelming his mind. He pulled himself away from her, his arms taking the weight of his body, and felt a strange internal tearing sensation in his leg. The pain did not increase, and part of Mike's panicked mind wondered if there was a ceiling to pain, an upper limit, and that however much it tried to fill a body it would never overflow that level.

Joanna was hauling at the knife now and suddenly his leg felt warm and wet. The blade ripped free and for a minute she paused over him, dripping knife in one hand, smears of blood on her face and chest. He knew what she'd done – crippled him, immobilised him. She meant to return him to the blaze.

She sat back on her knees, recovering her breath. Mike was conscious of a rising pain below his waist that spiked whenever he made to move his leg. He didn't know what had been severed in his calf, what web of muscles or strands of ligament had been sliced by that blade, but the knife had done its work.

He watched as Joanna stood, slowly, painfully. Then he had at least hurt her too. The blood on her body looked black in the dark, like the war paint of some tribal shaman. She raised the knife to the sky and opened her mouth to call for her friends.

And no words came out. She coughed, made to call again, but the only sound to leave her lips was a croak, a whisper. She looked with horror at Mike.

I killed her voice box, thought Mike. He remembered the feeling of that soft skin clamped in his hand, his thumb dug into the hollow of her throat. The wild, flailing punch which had robbed her of breath. *I wanted to kill her. But I just killed her voice.* A hysterical smile tugged at his mouth. *Try playing the flute now.*

She made to speak again, to put her beautiful voice into the world, to have it carry on the charged air of the field. But there was only the whisper, the wheeze of her damaged throat. Mike thought of the goat, of its last bubbles of life gurgling through the maw in its neck. It had bucked in his arms and kicked and twitched till well after it was dead, and he looked at the woman standing over him. She was still dangerous. She was still able to buck, to kick, to kill.

He pushed himself up on his arms. The muscles in his core ached but the discomfort was lost in the pain of his injuries. Joanna looked down at him and he met her eyes. He saw the hate in them, saw how his death had evolved in her heart from something ceremonial to something personal. He saw her hand tighten around the dagger, saw as she turned to come at him once more, to finish him off.

He kicked at her with his left foot. He felt as if his ankle had been knocked around at one hundred and eighty degrees, but the kick landed. It was weak, desperate, but it unbalanced her, and Mike flailed with his arms, pulling her down to the floor.

He had to keep her there, had to use his weight to pin her down. If she got up she would have manoeuvrability, she would have the advantage. She would kill him. He fought her, hands around hers, battling for the knife. He was stronger, heavier, but she was healthier, less hurting.

The dagger dropped to the ground, bouncing off the hard dirt. They both grabbed for it; she nimbler, he anchored by his crippled legs. They tangled, wrestled, but Mike couldn't reach the knife, not without lunging for it. Joanna would reach it first. And she would maim him till he prayed for the death the bonfire would bring.

He gripped her round the waist as she writhed and reached. Her fingertips brushed the handle of the dagger, and the sight fuelled Mike's last bid for victory.

He yanked her back and she fell into him, white gold hair filling his face and mouth. He reached around, grabbed her face, pulled her away, and rolled onto her, crushing the air out of her body. Her hands batted at him but his dead legs stopped him from pulling away, and he threw his fists into her face. After a few seconds, her hands stopped grabbing for him.

Mike gasped, deep from his lungs. Joanna wasn't moving. He pulled himself off her, reached for the knife and clenched it in his fist. Her face was covered by hair and he pushed it away.

Her pale face was bloodied; her nose looked

broken. He might have killed her but for small bubbles of blood that popped from her nostrils. He bent closer. Thin breaths hissed from between her lips.

He looked at the knife in his hand, and down at Joanna.

A part of him considered using the knife, plunging it into her heart, but he wouldn't do it. Not in cold blood. A part of him felt repulsed by the broken woman lying before him, repulsed at himself. He'd fought for his life, but he'd never hurt a woman before. Not like this.

There were sounds around him; movements, and Mike looked up, holding the knife out as if to defend himself.

Of course they saw us, he thought. *They may not have heard us but they would have seen us.* Broken images, visions of the wheat shaking a diabolic dance around their struggle, flashed in his mind. He saw that their fight had flattened the wheat around them into a circle. Then he was overtaken by a pulsing, hot sensation from his stabbed leg. He moaned out loud and felt his eyes water, spilling down his cheeks.

Around him, the figures appeared. Some carried scythes, others were unarmed. Mike raised the dagger, a futile attempt to intimidate them. Who was he kidding? Any one of them could overpower him now. This was it. This was the end.

One of the masked figures approached, and knelt by Joanna. Mike watched as the scythe was transferred to its left hand, and its right, a large hand, fingers like fat sausages, touched her face. Its fingers stayed over her mouth and nostrils as if checking for shallow breaths.

Mike saw her eyelids flicker.

The masked man looked at Mike. Beyond the antlered veil, Mike saw familiar eyes, eyes that were to be found in a familiar chubby face. He raised the knife again. The man looked away, back at Joanna, then nodded at the other figures.

He wanted to speak, to challenge them, to beg them, but no words would come. He was beyond anything but the most primal of movements. He watched as two figures advanced into the flattened circle, but rather than haul him up they stopped by Joanna. He saw her flickering eyelids blink and open properly as she was pulled up to her feet, and a mask of fear appeared on her face. She opened her mouth to speak, to scream, but no words came out; only a damaged whisper that was lost in the rustling of the wheat as she was carried through the field towards the crescent-shaped fire.

Mike could feel his body fading. He'd used up everything, everything he had, to survive. Now his vision blurred, doubled, and one of his eyes seemed to see everything in monochrome.

I'm blacking out, thought Mike. He saw the large figure with the antler mask approach him, bend down before him. He felt his fist lose its grip on the knife, felt the handle stick for a second on the curing blood, then peel away to hit the floor.

Over now, thought Mike, and there was no capacity for fresh terror in his shell of a body. He let himself slide into unconsciousness, escape into that void. *Over now.*

IX

For many minutes, Mike didn't open his eyes.

He let himself rest, pushing away any thoughts that tried to filter into his head. He burrowed further into the gauzy cocoon of sleep that for the most part still enveloped him. There was something just outside his mind's eye, flitting in his peripheral vision, but he turned from it. It wasn't hard. It was as if his mind wanted to forget.

My wife, he thought. *I want to wake up beside...*

Eventually, his eyes slid open, and began to focus.

He was in an unfamiliar room – or was he? Something in the plan of the place did ring a bell; the position of the bed, the door, the window. It wasn't his bedroom, wasn't his room at – at –

Harvest House.

Mike sat upright, felt pains up and down his body. He'd been here before; had woken up here on the night of...

Thoughts spiralled in from the sidelines of his memory. His stomach clenched as he remembered it all; the field, the pit, the goat (here his stomach roiled again and a pang of guilt stabbed him in the chest), the bonfire, his escape through the wheatfield. He remembered Joanna, remembered fighting for his life down on the ground, amongst the thrashing stalks of the wheat crop.

He threw off the covers of the bed and looked down at himself. He was naked, and his body was covered in bruises, cuts and scratches. His muscles felt worked, as if he'd had a grueling gym session the day before. But it was his left leg that drew his eye. It had been wrapped in a bandage, bound tightly. Above his swelled ankle, a dark red patch marked the spot on his calf where Joanna had thrust in the knife.

A rush of disbelief coursed through Mike's being, replaced quickly with a dawning horror. It had happened; all of it. He'd been stabbed, nearly burned alive, nearly *murdered*. And he was still here, still in the village of Crookleton, still in Harvest House.

He had to escape.

He looked around for his clothes; there were none. *Of course not*. As if they'd make it in any way easy for him to get away.

His muscles hurt as he pulled himself to the edge of the bed. His right leg felt numbed, as if he'd been administered some local anaesthetic, and it dragged behind his torso.

A potion, he remembered, from a lifetime ago.

He lugged his right leg over the side of the bed. His left felt fine; fine but for a swelled, tight sensation in his ankle. He tried to stand but his injuries undid him; his legs wouldn't take his weight. He pulled himself up the corner post of the bed to look out of the window.

Outside, the sky was blue-grey, and dark grey clouds floated before a pale sun. The day had a cold hue; there was nothing of summer's warmth in it. Mike looked down at the field.

Where he remembered a sea of golden wheat flowing in the breeze, now the field was flat and stubbly. There was nothing left of the circles, though he saw a blackened patch towards the field's adjacent border. *The bonfire.* A memory returned to him, a vision seen through drooping lids and blackened eyes. A figure thrashing at the centre of a blaze, black smoke pouring into the sky.

A smell of fires, smoky and autumnal, hung on the air. Mike looked back at the sky. The clouds were dark; remnants of that inferno, he guessed. They glided away on the breeze, bidding farewell the field below.

They watch the circles.

No more circles now. Not since the harvest.

Mike dropped back onto the bed. He could hear sounds from downstairs, from somewhere in the house.

He had to get away. He had to call the police, get the whole village arrested if need be. Why had they left him alive? Why had they taken her, taken Joanna, to burn in his place?

Because I beat her, he thought, remembering her body passed out on the ground. He'd had the knife in his hand; he could have killed her. *Because they only needed one worthy sacrifice. And I won the right to live.*

Footsteps on the stairs. Mike looked around as if for somewhere to hide, but he couldn't move, couldn't get away from the bed. He was as good as crippled.

The footsteps stopped outside the door, and a moment later it opened.

Reece walked in, carrying a tray.

'Mike. I thought I heard you up.'

Mike stared at him. As he looked at Reece, he saw a figure in a black cloak and a painted mask, antlers branching up from its crown.

'Why I am here?' he started. 'What am I doing here? Why do you need me?'

Reece placed the tray down on a coffee table.

'You're staying here, Mike. You stayed another night.'

Mike looked at him in disbelief. Reece looked back. After a few moments, he broke the silence.

'Think you might have taken a fall from your bike. During the Festival. We brought you back here; it was all we could do.'

Mike looked down at himself.

'The field,' he said. 'I saw you. All of you. I know what happened.'

Reece remained quiet, as if weighing his words and packaging them before delivering them to his mouth.

'The Festival is over now, Mike. All done. I think you'll find you'll be staying here a little longer, though.'

'You can't –' Mike couldn't finish; couldn't decide how to. *You can't be serious. You can't keep me here. You can't deny what happened.* 'Let me go,' he said, finally.

'No.' Reece remained standing. He looked at Mike and nodded slightly. 'You're safe here.'

They stared at each other. Mike understood – thought he understood – the significance of Reece's words.

I am safe. They wish me no harm. Not... anymore.

'The Festival is over,' repeated Reece.

They don't need me anymore. They've taken the sacrifice they need.

'And you will stay here until you are healed.' Mike held Reece's gaze until the fat man looked away. 'If you need anything, just shout.' He clunked the door shut behind him.

Mike sank back onto the bed. He felt an odd sense; not only relief, although relief was a core part of it. It was more like contentment.

He looked at the tray Reece had placed beside the bed. A jug of water, a small loaf of bread. Mike poured himself a glass of water; his mouth was dry. It tasted cool and refreshing.

It would be a day or two before the swelling in

his ankle went down, he was sure. From there he could hop about on his other leg – the one with the wound. Then he could be on his way back to...

To Ellen. Yes.

Strange. He had had to think hard for his wife's name, dredging it from some murky zone in his tired mind.

He looked down at himself. He was hurt; bruised, bloodied. His body must just be tired, pushed to an extreme. He could be forgiven such a small moment of absent-mindedness.

He gulped another mouthful of water then put the glass down. He could feel his body sinking into itself, as if the strain of being awake was too much for it, and he let his eyes close too. He felt light, and the bed beneath him felt soft, so soft he could submerge into the very fabric of it.

He pictured his body drifting further down, but his soul stayed where it was, as if it were lighter than that mortal shell. He felt that consciousness rise, up from the bed, up to the ceiling.

It was a dream. Of course it was. He was asleep again; his body couldn't sustain any amount of activity after what he'd been through. He remembered another dream, something about darkness and fires and running, a dream brought to him on the golden breeze through his open window. But it was distant now and the more he sought to remember it the farther away it flew, until he could remember nothing of it. There was only the sensation of rising, rising beyond the confines of Harvest House and into the sky above. He could see the shape of the village, two arms enclosing the field at its centre. Although the field was cut, harvested to stubs, he knew where the circles had been, could see them the same as he could still see the sun or moon when they dipped behind cloud. He had a bird's eye view, he watched the circles.

He woke at night. Something told him he had been asleep for more than a day. He felt heavy, as if his body had not moved for hours upon hours.

Moonlight filtered through the open window. Mike sat up. He could see the moon now, pale and huge, high in the sky. He slid himself to the edge of the bed and stood up, gently, and held onto the window sill.

He could see the field below. A few lights in the windows of houses dappled the night down either side of the field, but it was the moonlight that lit the world in whites and blacks and greys.

Mike stood and watched for many minutes. Then he turned from the window.

He saw something like a long black coat hanging on the back of the door. His legs were weak but they walked him to the other side of the room, and he wrapped the coat around his naked body. It was soft and the hood bunched at his neck.

The bedroom door opened with barely a sound and Mike padded out. He held the banister as he made his way down the stairs. There were lights on in the reception room and, as he entered, he saw a dark shape rise from a chair by the window.

Reece looked Mike up and down.

'Awake at last,' he said.

Mike looked down at himself.

'Yes,' he said. Then: 'I think I'm ready to go.'

For the first time, Reece's mouth twitched into something like a smile.

'I can see that.' He walked over to Mike, put an arm around his shoulders. 'Let's get you ready.'

The stairs creaked beneath their feet. Reece led him back to his room then left him, reappearing with a pile of clothes.

'Leave that with me,' he said, as Mike stripped off the long black coat. 'You won't need it yet. Not where you're going.'

Mike redressed in his own things, and Reece handed him his rucksack.

'The rest,' he said. Mike slung the pack onto his shoulder, and followed Reece back down the stairs. The chubby man opened the door for him.

'Thank you,' said Mike. 'Thanks for having me.'

'You're welcome.' Reece held out a hand, and Mike shook it. 'I hope you work it out with your wife.'

'Thank you.' Mike turned to the driveway. The moon was bright. He could see perfectly.

'Until next September,' said Reece.

Mike turned back.

'Until then,' he said.

He stepped through the doorway and began to

walk, with only the faintest trace of a limp. Within minutes, he had left Harvest House behind him.

A Note on the Illustrations

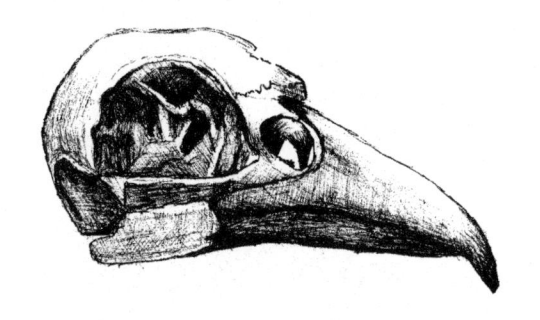

The illustrations in this book are the work of Neil Elliott, an artist based in Sussex.

Neil has combined his superlative talents with a pencil with a tireless effort to capture the themes and motifs of *Harvest House*. It is my pleasure to showcase some of the additional illustrations he has produced whilst working on the book.

This is not your country
This is not your land
For here we keep the old beliefs
You would not understand

This is not your country
These are not your ways
For all the year our covenant
Holds sway over this place

Fig 1.

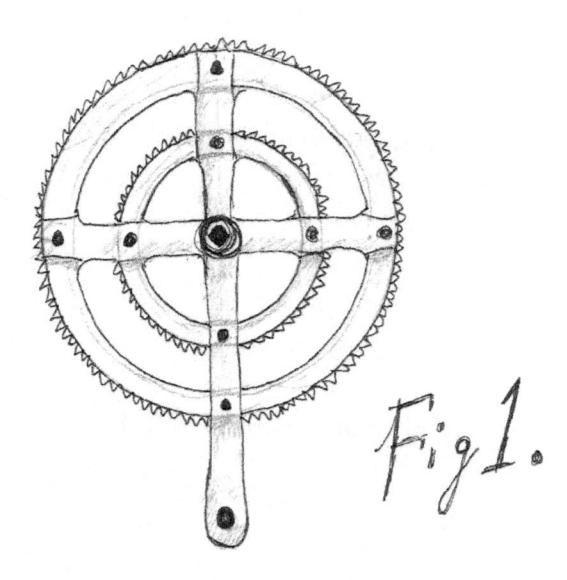

This is not your country
We are not your folk
We know the ways of sacrifice
By soil, scythe and smoke

This is not your country
These are not your fields
The landscape is our temple here
'Midst stalk and rig we kneel

Fig 2.

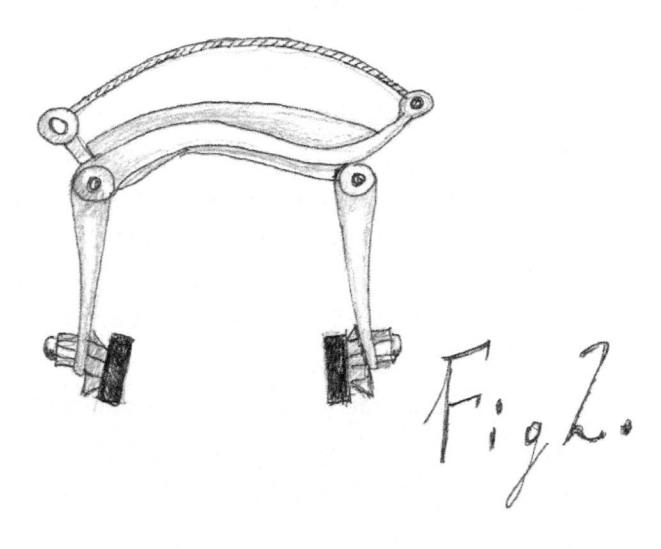

This is not your country
This is not your season
You find no gods to rule you, just
Tradition to believe in

This is not your country
This is not your land
For here we keep the old beliefs
You would not understand

Fig 3.

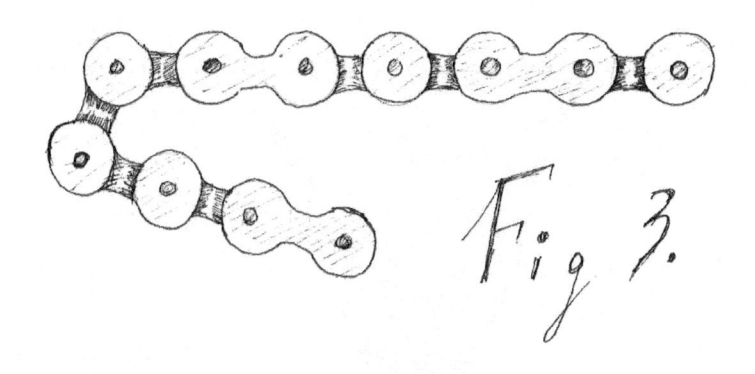

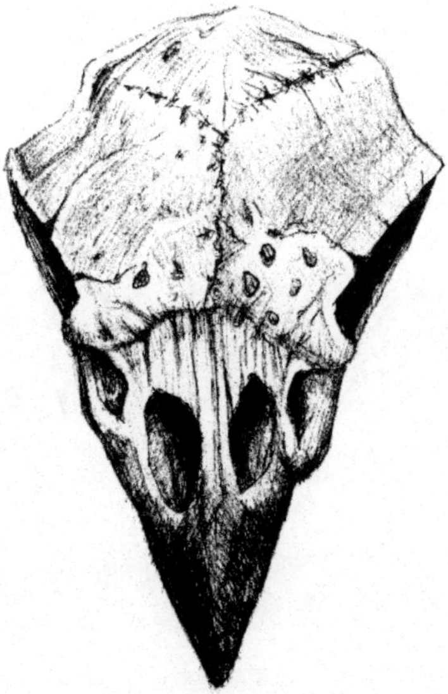

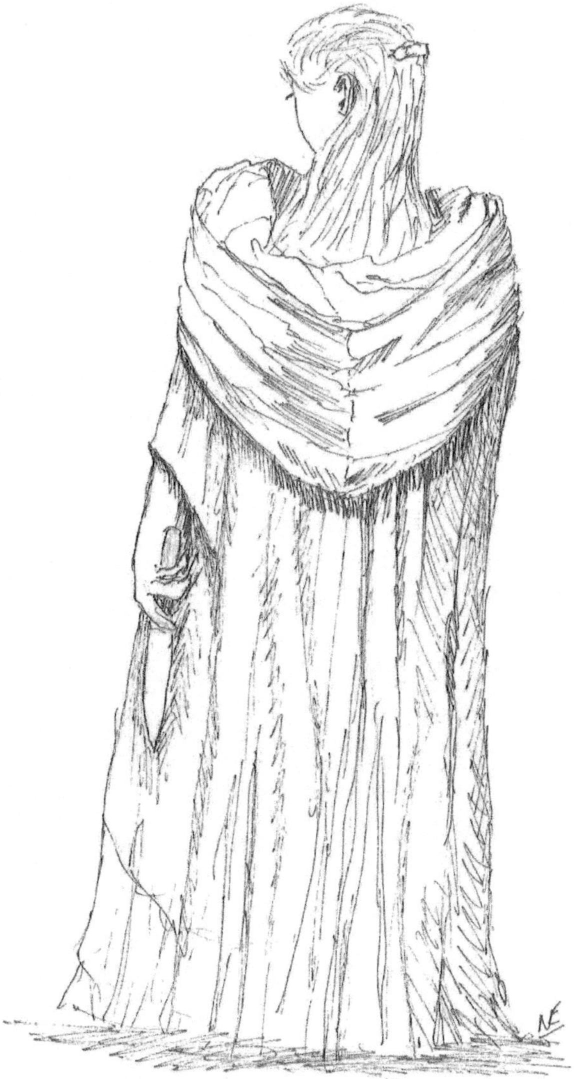

About the Author

Liam Smith enjoys writing quietly, drumming loudly and dressing in black. He has been known to haunt the South Coast of Sussex, bringing twisted tales and gothic performance poetry to unsuspecting audiences.

Liam hopes you enjoyed reading these stories as much as he enjoyed writing them. If you feel like contacting Liam, visit his website at:

www.liamsdesk.co.uk

or find him on Facebook or Twitter:

@HoraceCSmith

He would love to hear from you.

Printed in Great Britain
by Amazon